ISBN 978-0-243-47530-8
PIBN 10800840

English
Français
Deutsche
Italiano
Español
Português

www.forgottenbooks.com

Mythology Photography **Fiction**
Fishing Christianity **Art** Cooking
Essays Buddhism Freemasonry
Medicine **Biology** Music **Ancient
Egypt** Evolution Carpentry Physics
Dance Geology **Mathematics** Fitness
Shakespeare **Folklore** Yoga Marketing
Confidence Immortality Biographies
Poetry **Psychology** Witchcraft
Electronics Chemistry History **Law**
Accounting **Philosophy** Anthropology
Alchemy Drama Quantum Mechanics
Atheism Sexual Health **Ancient History**
Entrepreneurship Languages Sport
Paleontology Needlework Islam
Metaphysics Investment Archaeology
Parenting Statistics Criminology
Motivational

PLAYS BY PHILIP BARRY

THE ANIMAL KINGDOM

A Comedy

BY

PHILIP BARRY

SAMUEL FRENCH

NEW YORK   LOS ANGELES

SAMUEL FRENCH Ltd.   LONDON

MANUFACTURED IN THE UNITED STATES OF AMERICA
BY THE VAIL-BALLOU PRESS, INC., BINGHAMTON, N. Y.

TO GILBERT MILLER AND LESLIE HOWARD

"THE ANIMAL KINGDOM" was first produced by Gilbert Miller and Leslie Howard at the Broadhurst Theatre in New York City on January 12, 1932. It was directed by Gilbert Miller and the settings were designed by Aline Bernstein.

CHARACTERS

Rufus Collier
Tom Collier
Cecelia Henry
Daisy Sage
Joe Fisk
Franc Schmidt
Owen Arthur
Grace Macomber
Richard Regan

Action and Scene

The action of the Play takes place in the course of about eighteen months, last year and this. The Scenes are as follows:

Act One

Scene 1. At Tom Collier's, in Connecticut. An evening in April.

Scene 2. At Daisy Sage's, on Thirty-eighth Street. Later the same evening.

Act Two

Scene 1. At Tom Collier's. An evening in January.

Scene 2. At Daisy Sage's. An afternoon in May.

Act Three

Scene 1. At Tom Collier's. A Sunday morning in October.

Scene 2. At Tom Collier's. Later the same evening.

ACT ONE

ACT ONE

SCENE I

The library of TOM COLLIER'S *house in the country near New York. About seven o'clock on an April evening, two years ago.*

The library is a fair-sized, comfortable room in a small, partially converted farmhouse, situated in a countryside which is neither fashionable nor suburban. There is an entrance from the hall at Left and one into the dining-room through another hall at Back Right. In the center wall at Back, there is a fine old fire place, framed with pine panelling. The side walls are of white plaster, windows in the one at Right, with bookshelves around them. At Left, a small staircase leads to the upper floor. The furniture, of no particular period, is well chosen and, in the case of chairs and sofa, invitingly comfortable. It is a cheerful room, now filled with the late evening sun.

Upon the sofa, sits OWEN ARTHUR. *In an easy chair, turned away from him, is* RUFUS COLLIER. CECELIA HENRY *is seated in a straight chair beside a table at Right Center.* OWEN *is about thirty-five, well built, well dressed, agreeable looking.* RUFUS *is in his early fifties, small, slight and gray. He wears silver-rimmed spectacles, which add to his picture of himself as the man of decision.* CECELIA *is twenty-eight, lovely of figure, lovely of face, beautifully cared for, beautifully presented.*

3

For some moments, all sit staring in front of them, saying nothing. Finally OWEN *clears his throat, waits a moment, and without turning, ventures:*

OWEN

There's quite a fine view from the hill behind the house. (*A silence.*)—Or did I tell you that?

RUFUS

Yes.

OWEN

Sorry.

[*Another silence. Then* CECELIA *speaks.*

CECELIA

You've *really* never been here before?

RUFUS

I?

CECELIA

Yes.

RUFUS

Never.

CECELIA

It seems a little strange.

RUFUS

I've never been asked before. (*He glances about him.*) What anyone wants with a place at the end of the world like this, is beyond me anyhow.

OWEN

I make it in less than an hour, as a rule.

RUFUS

Oh, you come often, do you?

OWEN

Fairly. I find there's nothing like it after a stiff week in Court. I'm a new man since Friday.

RUFUS

You seem to be a fixture with him. I'm surprised he hasn't given you the go-by, as well.

OWEN

I'm too fond of him. I won't allow it.

RUFUS

But you're well-off, you work hard, you live like a gentleman—his natural enemy, I should say.

OWEN

We make few demands on each other. And he knows how I love this place.

RUFUS

But there's nothing *here*! No social life, no—

OWEN

Exactly.

CECELIA

His press is in the Village, isn't it?

RUFUS

Press? What press?

CECELIA

The Bantam Press. (*He stares.*) You know—for books.

o it's publishing now, is it?

ᴸ

nk it has been, for some time.

(*to* OWEN)

's it going, do you know?

well. Last year he only lost something li]

ɪn't tell me!
rises and goes to the window.

ᴸ

re not awfully fond of your son, are you
ɛr?
US *turns to her.*

—I beg your pardon—you said your
-?

ᴸ

y. Cecelia Henry.

Henry, if you had spent the time and n
ɛffort I have to make that young man r
ɪe is and what he ought to be doing in the
ᴡ long have you known him?

ᴸ

ɪomparatively new, I'm afraid.

RUFUS (*to* OWEN)

Perhaps, from longer experience, you might en-lighten her.

OWEN

I presume what Mr. Collier means is that on ordinary terms, Tom doesn't seem to have got very far.

CECELIA

There's still time, isn't there?

RUFUS

Thirty-one—thirty-two in October—and he's wasted his life from the cradle.

CECELIA

It must have been pathetic to see him wasting it at three.

RUFUS

I assure you, his genius for it showed even then. I send him to Harvard, and he lasts two years there. I send him to Oxford, and he commutes from Paris. I put him in the Bank, and he— (*He sighs pro-foundly.*)—The world at the feet of that boy, the whole world. And all he's ever done is to run from it.

OWEN

Tom has his own ideas about what he wants to do with his life. (RICHARD REGAN *has come into the room. He is about thirty-two, with the figure of an athlete, red hair, and a genial, ugly Irish face that appears at some time to have been thoroughly mauled. He wears dark trousers and a white linen*

jacket, and carries a slip of paper in his hand.)
—Yes, Regan?

REGAN

There's a radio-message came by phone for him.

OWEN

You can leave it here. I'll tell him.
[REGAN *folds the message and places it upon the table.*

REGAN

Right. (*He turns and beams upon them.*)—Everything satisfactory?

OWEN

Yes, thanks.

REGAN

Comfortable, Miss?

CECELIA

Quite, thank you.

REGAN

Like a drink, anyone?

RUFUS (*exasperated*)

No, no! Nothing! We were talking!

REGAN (*with a wave of his hand*)

Go right ahead. Make yourselves to home. He'll be along.
[*He goes out.* CECELIA *laughs.*

CECELIA

—The butler? But he's charming!

RUFUS

He looks like a prize-fighter.

OWEN

He was.

[RUFUS *begins to hover curiously about the radio-message, wanting to read it, not quite able to bring himself to.*

RUFUS

Why did he send me word to come out here tonight? Exceedingly important? Don't let anything interfere?

OWEN

I don't know. I found a message asking me to get Miss Henry at my Aunt's in New Canaan, and come back on the run. He had to go to town for something.

RUFUS

Well, I'll tell you what's in my mind—God knows I don't want it there.—That girl he's been living with for the last three years—

[OWEN *glances quickly at* CECELIA.

OWEN

Just a minute, Sir.

CECELIA

It's all right, Owen.

RUFUS

Good Lord, it's no secret, is it? (*To* CECELIA.) —You're not her, are you?

A

that I know of.

(*to* OWEN)

⟩ is she, anyhow? What is she?

n extremely nice girl—hard-working, talented.
draws for the fashion magazines, and very suc-
:ully.

irable.—Well, I believe he's got me out here to
me he wants to marry her—or has already.—
no doubt he'll bring her with him.

ously—can you see Tom marrying anyone?

n see her marrying him. It has happened before,
to better men.

ain he hovers about the radio-message.

was going to to them, it would have long before
Besides, she left for her magazine's Paris office
ɘ months ago, for an indefinite stay.

be she's coming back.—In fact, I'm certain that
: why we're here. It offers the perfect opportunity
ıt himself off finally and completely from the life
ʋas born to. I'm surprised he has missed it as
as he has. Well—I've stood for his rowdy friend-

ships, I've put up with his idleness, his ill-mannered insolence, his——

[CECELIA *rises and faces him.*

CECELIA

I'm sorry, Mr. Collier, but I'll have to ask you to let it go at that.

RUFUS

Ah? Why so?

CECELIA

—Because it so happens that *I'm* why we're here.

RUFUS

How's that?

CECELIA

It's me Tom's going to marry, and I've heard enough against him to last me quite a while.

[RUFUS *stares.* OWEN *starts forward.*

OWEN

—You that Tom's——?!—Good Lord, C, what are you talking about?

CECELIA

Marrying. On May first, to be exact. (*To* RUFUS.) He asked you out here to tell you, and, I imagine, to receive your good wishes. (RUFUS *still stares.*) —Thanks so much.

[*She reseats herself,* OWEN *continues to gaze at her, speechless.*

RUFUS

What did you say your name was? I'm sorry, but I——

CECELIA

Cecelia Henry. My mother was Cecelia Bond, of
Baltimore. She married Stephen Henry, also of Baltimore. Except for a few distant cousins, such as
Owen here, I'm alone now—poor, but quite respectable. Will it do?

RUFUS

Tom has very little of his own, you know.

CECELIA

It will be ample, thank you.

RUFUS (*after a moment*)

Miss Henry, I'm inclined to like you. I think you
have what I call "character."

CECELIA

Really? You're too kind.

RUFUS

You'll need it with him.

CECELIA

I don't agree with you. Tom is the most interesting,
most attractive man I've ever known. I consider
myself shot with luck. And you make me a little
tired with your abuse of him.

RUFUS

—Very loyal.

CECELIA

Not at all. I simply believe in him.—Not in his so-
called "past" perhaps—I'm not quite a fool—but
certainly in what's to be.

RUFUS

Faith is a beautiful thing.

CECELIA

I think so.

RUFUS

Well, if you can make a respectable citizen of Tom Collier at this date, you'll have nothing but praise from me, my dear.

[*He picks up the radio-message and draws it through his fingers.*

CECELIA

It seems not to occur to you that when Tom has someone who really understands him to work and care for—

OWEN

Understands him!

CECELIA

Yes. Completely. (*Again to* RUFUS.)—He'll make what you call "a citizen" of himself.

[RUFUS *adjusts his spectacles and reads the message.*

RUFUS

You think?

CECELIA

I know.—And if what you laughingly refer to as my "faith" is of any use to him—

RUFUS

"Love will conquer all." Yes, yes—of course— (*He*

sighs and refolds the message.)—But forgive me a few doubts.

[OWEN *leans forward.*

OWEN

Oh? How's that, Sir?

RUFUS

"Darling. Am coming back. Arrive on 'Paris' at eight tonight. Much love. Daisy."

[*He looks at* CECELIA. *There is a slight pause. Then:*

CECELIA

Well?

[RUFUS *rises, and regards her intently.*

RUFUS

—Yes, you seem to be a first-rate girl.

CECELIA

I've heard some rather agreeable things about *you,* now and then. It would be pleasant sometime to—

RUFUS (*smiling*)

—To see one or two of them? Well, my dear, perhaps some day you shall.—And now if you'll let me have Mr.—er—Mr. Arthur to myself for a moment— (*He moves toward the doorway.*)—There are a few dull but practical facts about—er—about your fiancé, I should like to— (*He turns to* OWEN.)—Would you mind?

[OWEN *moves to follow him.* RUFUS *goes out.*

CECELIA

Wait a minute, Owen, will you please?

[OWEN *stops and turns.*

OWEN

Well?

CECELIA

I'm sorry you had to learn about it so—abruptly.

OWEN

It doesn't matter much, does it?

CECELIA

I don't know.

OWEN

Perhaps I was supposed to hear it with little cries of pleasure.

CECELIA

The point is, that I intended to tell you on the way over, but somehow couldn't.

OWEN

I'm touched by your reluctance to deliver the blow.

CECELIA

Don't be nasty, Owen.

OWEN

It was kind of me to bring you together, wasn't it?

CECELIA

An inspiration. I'm sure I'm most grateful.

OWEN

I can't make it out. You aren't in the least the sort of girl I'd expect Tom to be interested in.
[*She laughs.*

CECELIA

Thanks!

OWEN

You know what I mean.

CECELIA

Perhaps it's the artist in him. You see, he has the charming illusion that I'm a real beauty.

OWEN

—And I *can't* make *you* out, either.

CECELIA

It's quite simple: I'm in love at last.

OWEN

Have you the remotest idea of what you're letting yourself in for?

CECELIA

I think so.

OWEN

I'm the one friend you and Tom have in common.

CECELIA

—But such a lovely friend, Owen. Don't ever leave me—us.

OWEN

There's not a taste, not an attitude—

CECELIA

Perhaps there will be. Give us time.

OWEN

C—how on earth did it happen?

CECELIA

Very suddenly, very sweetly.—Yesterday. (*He turns away.*) I'm sorry. You asked.
[*A moment. Then:*

OWEN

—I'll see what it is Mr. Collier wants, if you don't mind.
[OWEN *goes out.* CECELIA *looks after him for a moment, then removes her hat, seats herself in a large chair, hidden from the doorway, and thoughtfully lights a cigarette. A moment, then* TOM COLLIER *appears in the doorway,* REGAN *close behind him.* TOM *is in his early thirties, slim, youthful, with a fine, sensitive, humorous face. He carries several packages in his arms.*

TOM

Where are they?

REGAN

Well—they *were*.
[CECELIA *rises and turns.*

CECELIA

Hello, Tom.

TOM (*to* REGAN)

Take my hat. (REGAN *removes it from his head.*) Thanks. Now get out.

REGAN

I just wanted to tell you that—

TOM

Later.

[*He is gazing fondly at* CECELIA.

REGAN

But there's a—

TOM

Get, will you, Red?

[REGAN *goes out, murmuring:*

REGAN

—Radio-message come for you.

[*But* TOM *scarcely hears him. Suddenly he drops his parcels upon the table, goes to* CECELIA *and takes her in his arms.*

TOM

Darling, darling—

[*He is about to kiss her, but she averts her head.*

CECELIA

No. You're late. I'm furious with you.

TOM (*blankly*)

Late?

[*She looks at him for a moment, then smiles and kisses him lightly.*

CECELIA

There.—All right?

TOM

Terrible. I've taken up with a thrifty spinster.

CECELIA

It's all you deserve.

[*He laughs.*

TOM

How do you like it?—I mean the place.

CECELIA

I love it.

TOM

I call it "the house in bad taste."—Look out for taste, C. There's too much of it in the world. (*He goes to the packages on the table.*) See here—what I fetched from town for you.

CECELIA

What are they?

TOM

A celebration: good things to eat and drink.—Where are they? Father? Owen?

CECELIA

In the other room.

TOM

What do you think of Father?

CECELIA

Well—

TOM

Keep a civil tongue in your head.

CECELIA

It may take a little time.

TOM

You can learn to like him and beer together. Mothe
was the prize: you missed something, there. Fathe
means well, but you have to stand him off. Give hi
an inch, and he takes you home in his pocket. Di
you really say you'd marry me?
[*He slips her arm through his and leads her to*
chair.

CECELIA

I'm afraid I did.

TOM

Heaven help us both.—Just this one marriage pleas
darling. I haven't been very good about marriage.
was exposed to a very bad case of it as a baby. W
must make a grand go of it.

CECELIA

We shall, never you fear.
[TOM *smiles.* CECELIA *seats herself in the chair,* TO
upon the arm of it.

TOM

—Just do everything I say, and it will be all righ

CECELIA

—With pleasure.
[*He gazes at her.*

TOM

C, what a marvellous object you are. (*He picks u*
her hand, looks at it.) Look at those fine small bone
in your wrist.

CECELIA

What about them?

TOM

This— (*He kisses the wrist.*)
—You're so cunningly contrived.

CECELIA

What?

TOM

I say, you're put together on the very best princi-
ples.

CECELIA

I don't see so many blunders in you either, Thomas.

TOM

No, mine is entirely beauty of soul. Shall I tell you
about my soul, C?—With lantern-slides?

CECELIA (*softly*)

Put your arms around me, Tom.

[*He draws her to him and kisses her. Then:*

TOM

—Oh God, I feel good!

CECELIA (*in a breath*)

—So do I.

TOM

—Let's have all our good things together. (*He turns
and calls loudly:*) Red! Oh, Red! (*Then turns again
to* CECELIA.) That's a very good rule of life, darling:
all one's good things together.

CECELIA

Is it, dear?

[REGAN *appears beaming.* TOM *rises from the chair.*

REGAN

Hello. Not so loud.

TOM

—Glasses with ice, Red, and run all the way.

REGAN

O.K.

[*He goes out.* TOM *calls again:*

TOM

Owen? Father! (*Then turns and regards* CECELIA *once more.*) Oh, my lovely C—you lovely thing, you.

CECELIA

Stop it, Tom. You're really embarrassing me. I feel quite naked.

TOM

That's fine. (*He goes to her and draws two fingers gently across her cheek.*) It's such a fine binding, darling—such a good book. (RUFUS *re-enters, followed by* OWEN.) Hello, Father, hello, Owen—terribly nice you're here. You've met Miss Henry, Father?

RUFUS

I've had that pleasure, yes.

TOM

It *is* a pleasure.—How are the horses?

RUFUS

Do you care?
[TOM *laughs.*

TOM

Not a bit.

RUFUS

Then why ask?

TOM

Politeness.

RUFUS

You said five o'clock. It's seven.

TOM

Did I? Is it?—Listen,—you and Owen—I want to tell you what this is all about.

RUFUS

We know. We've heard.
[TOM *looks to* CECELIA.

CECELIA

He was abusing you so, I had to tell him.
[TOM *laughs delightedly.*

TOM

And it didn't discourage you?

CECELIA

On the contrary.

TOM

Stout heart. (*Then, gravely, to* RUFUS.) Why, thank you very much, Sir, but I think *I'm* the one to be

congratulated. Yes, indeed we are. Yes, I'm sure
we shall be. (REGAN *comes in with a tray of glasses
filled with ice.*) Oh—er—this is my father, Red.

REGAN

Glad to meet you, Sir.

[RUFUS *bows slightly.* REGAN *undoes one of the packages and produces a bottle of champagne.*

TOM

—And my fiancée, Miss Henry.

[*Bottle in hand,* REGAN *stares at him, puzzled.*

REGAN

Your—?

[*Then goes to* CECELIA, *seizes her hand, shakes it
warmly and goes out.* CECELIA *laughs.*

CECELIA

He is priceless!

TOM

A magnificent fellow, Red. We box every morning.
I gave him that ear—but you watch, I'll pay for
it. (*To* RUFUS.) *You* keep pretty fit, don't you, Father?

RUFUS

Quite. Do you mind?

TOM

I'm delighted. My only wonder is that some designing
woman doesn't snap you up. Look how C got me.
(*To* CECELIA.)—Like *rolling off a log, wasn't it?

CECELIA

Easier, much.

RUFUS

I keep my defenses well in line.

[TOM *laughs, and turns to* OWEN.

TOM

Did you hear what he said? (*To* RUFUS.)—Millions for defense, eh, Sir?—But not one cent for cab-fare. (REGAN *has come in again with the bottle, now opened, and is filling the glasses.*) That's the boy, Red. Pass them, will you? Then get dinner going. I could eat an ox. (REGAN *passes the glasses.* TOM *turns to* CECELIA.) Are you hungry too, Angel?

CECELIA

Simply famished.

TOM

Good. I like a girl who likes her food. Once I said to Daisy— (*He stops, waits a moment, then smiles and raises his glass.*) Well—here's how and why and wherefore—and you know where marriages are made. (*All drink.* REGAN *has a glass of his own, which he downs at a gulp.*)—Speaking of eating, I ran into Jim Winter—you know Jim, Owen—in town to-day. He wants me to go salmon-fishing in Canada in June. I think I'll take him up on it. I've never done it.—It sounds like great sport, eh, Red?

REGAN (*putting down his glass.*)

Did you get your radio, Tom?

TOM

What radio's that?

REGAN

There on the table.

[*He goes out.*

CECELIA

In June, did you say?

TOM

Yes. It won't be for long. (*He takes a swallow from his glass and puts it down.*) My, what a noble wine. (*He picks up the radio-message.*)—I'll be back in three weeks at the outside.

CECELIA

Then we'll be married in July.

TOM (*turning*)

July! You said May.

CECELIA

Not if you're going straight off on a trip.

[*There is a silence. He regards her soberly.*

TOM

—That's easy, then. I won't go.

CECELIA

Perhaps you'd better think it over.

TOM

No, darling. I don't have to.

CECELIA

All right, Tom. (*She smiles and raises her glass to him.*)—To May first.

[*All drink.* TOM *opens the radio-message, reads it*

and refolds it carefully. All are watching him. He thinks a moment, frowning, then turns to OWEN.

TOM

Owen—would you like to show Father the new bantam-cock?

[OWEN *rises and moves toward* RUFUS.

OWEN

The red one?—Right.—Will you come along, Sir?

[OWEN *goes out.* RUFUS *does not stir.* TOM *goes to him, and slips his arm through his.*

TOM

You must see him, Father. He's a beauty, that bird. He fights at the drop of a hat. (*He draws him toward the door,* OWEN *following.*)—Even if you don't drop it, he fights. I'm sure he'll be interested to meet you, too, Sir.

[*He withdraws his arm, and* RUFUS *goes out.* TOM *closes the door after him, hesitates a moment, then returns slowly to* CECELIA.

CECELIA

Don't tell me if you don't want to, Tom.

TOM

But I do. I intended to at the first opportunity any-how, and— (*He glances at the radio-message once again.*)—And it seems that suddenly here it is.

[*And puts it in his pocket.*

CECELIA

Am I to be a good soldier?

TOM

No. There's no need to be.—Though I'm sure you would be, if there were.

CECELIA

Thanks, dear.

TOM

C, for quite a long time I've known—known intimately—a girl who's been very important to me—

CECELIA

Yes.

TOM

—Who always will be very important to me.

CECELIA (*smiling*)

—That's harder.

TOM

It shouldn't be. Because it has nothing to do with you and me, not possibly.

CECELIA

I'm relieved to hear that.

TOM

In fact, as it stands, I think she'll be glad for us.

CECELIA

I hope she will.

TOM

I'm sure of it.—C, Daisy has done more for me than anyone in this world. She's the best friend I've got. I believe she always will be. I'd hate terribly to lose her. It's been a queer sort of arrangement—no arrangement at all, really. There's never been any idea of marriage between us. It's hard to explain what there has been between us. I don't believe it's ever existed before on land or on sea. Well—

[*He hesitates again.*

CECELIA

Is she attractive, Tom?

TOM

To me, she is. She's about so high, and made of platinum wire and sand.—You wouldn't like me half so well, if Daisy hadn't knocked some good sense into me.

CECELIA

Well, someone's done a good job.

[TOM *laughs.*

TOM

I'll tell her that. (*Then seriously.*) I sent her a long cable about us this morning. She couldn't have got it, because this— (*He taps his pocket.*) this is from the boat. She lands tonight.

CECELIA

I see.

TOM

I want to be sure that you understand it—understand it both ways. I'd rather not go—terribly deeply into it if you don't mind.

CECELIA

I don't, Tom.

We've been—everything possible to each other of
course, and—

ELIA

es, Tom.

ut at the same time, free as air. There's never been
ny responsibility to each other involved in it—

ELIA

can understand that.

an you, C? Because I never could.—Anyhow, that's
the way it's been.—We haven't been what you'd call
n love," for quite a long time, now, so—

ELIA (*smiling*)
oes she know that?

he knew it first. Well—I don't know what more
ere is to say about it, except that there's no rea-
n at all for you to worry, and—you won't, will
ou?

LIA
o, Tom. Not if you tell me I needn't.

do.—And finally, that I think she ought to know
e—news about us, pretty promptly.

LIA
s. Probably.

TOM

Is whatever I do about it all right with you?

CECELIA

Absolutely.

TOM

Thanks, C.

CECELIA

There's just one thing I'd like to ask. May I?

TOM

Why of course, darling. What?

CECELIA

Are you quite sure that—? (*She sees* OWEN *and* RUFUS *coming in.*)—Poor Mr. Collier. I'm sure you loathe chickens. I quite agree with you.

RUFUS

—Vicious little beast.

[REGAN *comes in beaming.*

REGAN

Come on, everyone! Dinner!

TOM

You haven't put the car away, have you?

REGAN

Say, how many hands have I got?

TOM

Don't. I'll need it.

[REGAN *goes out.* TOM *turns to his father.*

TOM

Father, I'm afraid I'll have to ask you to do the honors at dinner.

RUFUS

The—? Why? How's that?

TOM

I find I've got to go straight back to town.
[*A silence. Then:*

OWEN

But I thought this was to be a celebration.

RUFUS

I had the same impression.

TOM

I'm sorry: it can't be helped.

OWEN

Is it so important to go in just this minute, Tom?

TOM

Yes—unfortunately.
[RUFUS *is eyeing him shrewdly.*

RUFUS

Why? What's wrong?

TOM

Nothing at all. It's simply that someone's arriving from Europe. I've missed the landing, as it is.— (*To* OWEN.)—Someone I've known a long time, and am fond of.

OWEN

Oh, I see.

TOM (*to* RUFUS)

I must—well, the fact is, I must tell her my—my good news.

RUFUS

Now you listen to me—
[TOM *confronts him.*

TOM

—And it seems to me extremely important that I should do it at once. In fact, I can't do otherwise.
[RUFUS *bursts out:*

RUFUS

—You have the effrontery, the colossal bad taste, on the night of celebrating your engagement to a fine, trusting, loyal girl, to go from her—your fiancée—to your—to your—
[TOM *smiles.*

TOM

—The same old difficulty with words, eh, Sir?—Never mind. None of them would apply to Daisy.

RUFUS

It's beyond me. It's the confoundest impertinence I've ever known.

TOM (*smiling*)

But you see, for all your splendid moral judgments, you know so very little, Sir.

RUFUS

I suppose you know better.—If you leave her
night—

[TOM'S *smile vanishes.*

TOM

—Yes. Much better. (*He returns to* CECELIA,
her hand and kisses it lightly.)—Until tomo
my Angel.

[*He nods Good-night to* OWEN *and* RUFUS, *and*
out.

CURTAIN

ACT ONE

The sitting-room of DAISY SAGE's *flat, later the same night.*

DAISY's *flat occupies the top floor of an old house in the Murray Hill section of New York. The sitting-room also serves as a workroom for* DAISY. *Victorian in atmosphere, it is light and cheerful and has been decorated and furnished with an original and unerring feeling for the period. There is a fire place of simple design at Left and above it, a door opening into the bedroom. The entrance from the hall is up Right, and into the pantry, down Right. The sofa and chairs are fine old Victorian pieces, but comfortable in spite of it. There are three large windows in the back wall. Below them stands* DAISY's *work-table, piled with old magazines and sketches, drawing-boards, crayons, pens and pencils.*

Opposite TOM, JOE FISK *is seated. Between them stands* FRANC SCHMIDT, *violin under her chin, playing, and playing well, the concluding measures of a César Franck sonata. She is thirty, hard, rugged—in appearance more of a handsome farm-girl than musician.* JOE *is twenty-eight, fine Irish, nervous, intense, attractive.* FRANC *concludes the piece.*

35

JOE

Good!—You'll get there, Franc, if you work.

[*She returns the violin to its case and seats herself near them. She speaks with a slight German accent.*

FRANC

—Only I played it much better, much.

TOM

He just wasn't impressed, eh?

FRANC

Oh, yes.—He could book me on the Big Time, he said.

JOE (*incredulous*)

Vaudeville?

FRANC

—That is, if I would learn to roller-skate.

TOM

He wanted you to play on skates?

FRANC

—A sensation, he said.

[JOE *and* TOM *laugh with delight.* JOE *goes to her, takes her face between his hands and kisses her resoundingly upon the brow.*

JOE

My darling. My Dutch darling.

[*She brushes him aside.*

FRANC

Get away.

[JOE *calls in the direction of the bedroom:*

JOE

Daisy!—Did you hear about Franc and the booking-agent? (*He turns to* FRANC.) Where is she?

FRANC

—Probably taking another bath. It will be her third in six hours. That's what Europe does for you.

TOM (*indicating the pantry*)

—No. She's in there, I think.

JOE (*incredulously*)

Six hours! Two o'clock—?

FRANC

It's past it.

TOM

Will you two never go home?

JOE (*calling in the direction of the pantry*)

Daisy! We're going! (*To* TOM *and* FRANC.)—And I promised myself tomorrow I'd do a chapter or die.

TOM

How's it coming?

JOE

All right. At least it's begun to move.

TOM

What are you calling it?

JOE

"Easy Rider."

TOM

I like that.

FRANC

But what does it mean?

JOE

Good God, must it mean something? (*Again he calls.*)
Daisy!

FRANC

Yes. Your eyes have got smaller. You should get to
bed.

TOM

Both of you should—go on, will you?

JOE

Why?

TOM

I want to talk to Daisy.

JOE

Look here, Tom, what *is* on your mind?

TOM

I've got something to tell her.

JOE

News?

TOM

Yes.

JOE

Good news?

TOM

Very.

FRANC

Will she cheer?

TOM

I think so.

FRANC

Tell *us*, Tom!

TOM

No.

JOE

Why not?

TOM

I want to tell Daisy first. (*To* FRANC.) You know, I've been thinking: Johnny Bristed might get a concert for you.

FRANC

I don't want it yet. I'm not ready yet.

[*Again* JOE *calls.*

JOE

Daisy!

[DAISY SAGE *comes in from the pantry. She is twenty-six, slim, lithe, a stripling, but with dignity beyond her years and a rare grace to accompany it. In contrast to* CECELIA's *lush beauty, she is plain, but there is a certain style of her own, a presence, a manner that defies description. Instantly and lastingly attractive, like no one else one knows; in short "a person," an "original." She wears white pajamas that might as well be a dress, and carries a tray containing coffee and sandwiches.*

DAISY

—And furthermore, I don't believe I like France as much as I say I do. (*She puts down the tray.*)—And I don't for a minute believe that you're leaving.

FRANC

Joe must. So must I.

DAISY

—You stay the night, if you like, Tom. You can have my room. I've got all the work in the world to do before morning.

TOM

Why, thanks, Daisy, but—

DAISY

As you like. (*She seats herself, and gives them coffee and sandwiches.*) I had thirty sketches to get through on the boat.—Oh, what lovely intentions.

FRANC

Was it *rough?*

DAISY

No, but Pilard was on board and we spent hours on end in the smoking-room—talk, talk, and more talk.

JOE

He's a fine painter, Pilard.

TOM

He's a good painter.

JOE

Fine, I said.

TOM

—And last week Henry Collins could write. Hold on to your standards, Joe.

JOE

You teach me, will you, Master?

TOM

Collins' life shows in his work. He can't make up his mind whether he wants to be a writer or a man-about-town.

JOE

Why not both?

TOM

—Because, little Joe, his work is the only true mistress a real artist ever had. When he takes on the world he takes on a whore.

FRANC

That goes for all good men, not only artists.

DAISY

—But all good men are, aren't they?—Look at Tom. —You don't have to put marks on paper or dents in stone to qualify, do you?

TOM (*to* JOE)

—Yes, and pays for her favors with something a lot more precious than twenty dollars left on the mantelpiece.

[JOE *reflects.*

JOE

I had twenty dollars once. Now, when was it?

DAISY

There's a statue in Florence that made me think of you, Tom.

[TOM *laughs.*

TOM

Me! How?

DAISY

It's a David by Donatello.

TOM

You mean with the curls and the derby hat?

DAISY

That's right!

[TOM *shakes his head.*

TOM

—No David, me. I'm just the no-account-boy. Ask Father—he'll tell you.—Hand me another sandwich, Joe.

[JOE *gives him one.*

JOE

No-account, is it?—You've done more for people than any one man I know.

TOM

Why thanks, Joe.—It's not true, of course, but thanks.

JOE

And done it in the damndest, most unassuming way I've ever heard of.

TOM

Oh, go to hell, will you?

JOE (*to* FRANC)

I could name a dozen first-class talents that, if *he* hadn't nosed 'em out, would have—

TOM

Say, are you two going to hang around here all night?

JOE

We haven't seen her either you know.

[FRANC *puts down her cup.*

FRANC

I must teach you again how to make coffee, darling.

DAISY

Your country's the one, Franc.

FRANC

Ach! There is no more new music in Germany today than there is here.

JOE

I thought there was plenty here.

FRANC

Like what?—If someone goes— (*She hums the opening bar of the "Rhapsody in Blue."*)—at me again, I shall become mad.

[DAISY *gazes at the bulging brief-case on the floor beside the work-table. Her smile fades.*

DAISY

Oh, that work!—Look at it.

TOM

Is there much of it?

DAISY

At least eight hours.

JOE

I wish we could help.

TOM

—You can. Good-night, Joe.

DAISY

—And Briggs was at the dock.

TOM

I didn't get your radio till seven.

DAISY

That didn't matter. Anyhow I hate being met. Anyhow, I tell myself I do. Briggs was frantic. Apparently they've held the presses for two days.

TOM

You're a bad girl.

DAISY

I'm a scoundrel. I swore it would be on his desk at nine. I'll be lucky if I'm through by noon.

[JOE *laughs, and rises.*

JOE

Urge us to stay once more and we may give in.— Come along, Franc. I'll see you across the hall.

[FRANC *rises and takes up her violin-case.*

FRANC

—It is good to have you back, too, Tom. You are better than all of us, but Daisy. She is better than best. Between you, you stir up our lazy bones, you hold us together, you bind our wounds. You two are the—ach!—my blood is turned to beer.—Auf wiedersehen. Good-night.

[*She goes out.*

JOE

I'll drop in tomorrow afternoon about five, if I can.

DAISY

Fine. I ought to be up by then.

[*She follows* FRANC *into the hall.*

JOE (*to* TOM)

Will you be here?

TOM

I'm afraid I'll have to go to the country.

JOE

Shun the country. Things come out of the ground there in Spring.

[*He goes out.* TOM *is alone for a moment. Then* DAISY *re-enters.*

DAISY

—Love them as I do, I thought they'd never go.

TOM

So did I.

[*She puts her arms around him and looks up at him.*

DAISY

Hello, you dear Tom.

TOM

Hello, Daisy.
[*She kisses him lightly.*

DAISY

Now it seems I haven't been away at all. (*And leaves his arms.*) Oh, it's grand to be back!

TOM

It's grand having you.—Was the trip really all that you hoped it would be?

DAISY

It was better.—If only you'd been along. Oh Tom —the pictures! I got drunk on them every day, twice a day.

TOM

I was sure you would.

DAISY

And at night when the galleries were closed I sat around and dreamed of them.—The silly contempt I always pretended to have for painting—self-protection, of course—the stuff *I* draw.

TOM

But some of it's good.

DAISY

You're right, my boy. Some of it is. (*She goes to the table and picks up a portfolio.*) Look—full— sketches.—And not a dress, a hat, a pajama among them. A market-wagon—the angle of a doorway—an open trunk. A melon cut in half—three glasses and a corkscrew—all manner of funny objects. Oh Tom, two of the most exciting things have happened to me! Not one—two! (*She moves toward the sofa.*) Come—sit down—

TOM

What are they?

DAISY

I'm bursting with them. (*She makes room for him beside her on the sofa, looks at him lovingly, smiles contentedly, touches his arm.*) Good, this—isn't it?

TOM

But what, Daisy? Did you fall in love with Pilard?

DAISY

Well I should say not! (*She laughs.*) Pilard! (*Then.*) What's that? (*From the distance the strains of a violin are heard, playing variations on the scales.*) Oh—Franc. Still working.—Guess what I found in my room when I came in? (*He looks at her questioningly. She laughs.*)—It seems the Swede maid Franc got me doesn't approve of you:—Four shirts, three socks, five ties and a razor, all done up in a great big white handkerchief.

TOM

You'd better go back to colored ones.—Maids, I mean.—

DAISY

—Remember Gladys?

TOM

Remember Hannah?

DAISY

Remember Marietta? (*They laugh together happily. She slips her arm through his, and for a moment drops her head upon his shoulder.*) Oh Tom, God love you.

TOM

God love you, my dear. (*For a moment there is silence, except for the sound of* FRANC'S *violin. Then she raises her head and they speak simultaneously.*) Daisy—

DAISY

Darling— (*She laughs.*) What?

TOM

No—you tell me—

DAISY

Well, my heavy sledding ought to be over in a few weeks—by the first of May, anyway. What have you got on the fire—much?

TOM

Yes. A great deal. The fact is—

DAISY (*in a rush*)

—Work night and day until May. Then come to Mexico for a month with Daisy. I'm dying to go. Pilard was full of it. I know it's what I need for awhile, because—well, first—oh, I feel like a fool.

You mustn't breathe a word of it. (*He shakes his head.*)—Tom, I think I can paint.

TOM

But that's no surprise. I've always thought if only you'd—

DAISY (*quickly*)

Then you've always been wrong!—It's new. It's since these two months.—I believe that if I work my eyes out, and my fingers to the bone, someday I may paint.—You must be hard with me—no parties— no hell-raising—*work*.—And you mustn't let me show until you know I'm ready to. Is that agreed?

TOM

All right.

DAISY

You have a funny instinct about such things. I count on you.—As for the second thing—(*She hesitates.*) —You know—suddenly I feel shy with you. (*She rises.*) I don't like it. I don't like it a bit.

TOM

We've—it's been a long time.
[DAISY *goes again to the work-table.*

DAISY

Too long.—Perhaps I'd better wait to tell you the second thing.

TOM

No. Tell me now.

DAISY

Oh, my dear—what's wrong with us? Come here to me. (*He goes to her, takes her hands in his.*) That's better. Now I don't feel it so much. (*But still she looks at him anxiously. Finally she releases her hands, turns and fumbles among her work-materials, picks up a pencil.*)—These are German pencils. They can't touch ours. You'd think they could, but they can't. Give me a "Venus-6B," every time. (*She stares fixedly at the pencil for another moment, then puts it down and turns to him.*) You're a free man, Tommy. You always have been, with me. No questions asked. But please, Mexico in May together, because listen—No! Don't look at me. Look the other way— (*He averts his head. She goes on, rapidly.*) —I stayed three days with the Allens at Vevey and they've got the sweetest small boy about two and I got crazy about him and I want one, I want one like the devil. I'm crazy for one, and would you please be good enough to marry me, and—

TOM

Daisy, I—!

DAISY

Oh, it needn't be terribly serious!—It's not a life-sentence—just for a short while, if you like—it'd be such a dirty trick on him, if we didn't.—After I get my stuff through for the June issue—then Mexico for a month—I love you so much, I was a fool ever to think I didn't, and—ah, come on, Tom—be a sport—. (*She is breathless.*)— Give me a cigarette—
[*But he does not.*

TOM

Daisy—

DAISY (*quickly*)

All right. No go. Let's forget about it. What a foul necktie that is. The colors are awful.

TOM

Daisy, I—Oh God, God Almighty—

DAISY

Well, what is it? (*He covers her hand with his.*) —You're going to tell me something terrible.—What is it?

TOM

I'm going to be married.

DAISY (*incredulously*)

To be—?!
[*Then silence. She averts her head.*

TOM

Listen to me, darling, listen: you don't really care so much. You can't. It's simply that we—you and I— after all this time, naturally we'd feel—

DAISY

It must have happened pretty quickly.

TOM

It did. A month ago we hadn't even met. It was—

DAISY

You can spare me the details, please. I don't even want to know who she is.

[*He moves away from her.* FRANC'S *violin begins to be heard again.*

TOM

—Her name is Cecelia Henry.

DAISY

It sounds familiar. I've heard or read that some-where. Where?—Well, well, will wonders never cease? —If I'd thought you were in a marrying mood, I might have thrown my own—(*She picks up a small, limp hat from the table.*)—could you call it a hat?—in the ring a bit sooner. (*She drops the hat upon the table.*)—Behold, the Bridegroom cometh—and no oil for my lamp, as usual.—A foolish virgin, me—well, foolish, anyway.—When's it to be? Soon?

TOM

—About the first of May, we planned.

DAISY

I seé.—Of course, in that event Mexico *would* be out, wouldn't it?

TOM

—But I never dreamed you'd—oh God, I feel so awful.

DAISY

Does she know about us?

TOM

Yes.

DAISY

Honest Tom.

TOM

Oh, shut up.

DAISY

Remember me, Tom.

TOM

Oh my dear—as if ever in this world I—(*Suddenly, fearfully.*) Daisy!—There's to be no nonsense about not seeing each other as friends again, or any of that, you know—

DAISY

No?

TOM ,

No. We're grown-up human beings. We're decent and we're civilized. We—

DAISY

But there *will* be that nonsense. Oh yes—there'll be that, all right.—"Cecelia Henry"—Now I know where it was!

[*She picks up a magazine and begins to run through it.*

TOM

—But I don't understand it. I don't see why we shouldn't. I thought for a long time we'd been out of danger so far as—well, so far as—

[*He cannot finish it, but* DAISY *can.*

DAISY

—Wanting each other goes?

TOM

But haven't we?

DAISY

Speak for yourself, Tom.

[*He looks at her, waits a moment, then speaks.*

TOM

—You too, Daisy.—You first, I thought.

DAISY (*slowly, thoughtfully*)

It's true, that side of it was never so much to us, was it? Not in comparison—not after those first crazy months. But I thought that was natural. I was even glad of it—glad to find it was—other needs that held us together. (*She looks away.*)—Closely— without claims—not a claim—but so closely. (*A moment. Then suddenly, sharply.*) Tom—do you have to marry her?

TOM

I want to marry her.

DAISY (*into the magazine*)

I was just thinking—perhaps you simply want her— want her most awfully.

TOM

It's more than that, much more.

DAISY

I don't see how you can tell quite yet.—For all our big talk, we still belong to the animal kingd—(*She stops and looks closely at a photograph in the magazine.*) Here she is!—Oh, these neat, protected women. I've drawn so many of them, dressed so many more.

TOM

If you knew her—

DAISY

But I don't, you see.—(*She holds the magazine at arm's length, gazing at the photograph.*) Such a pretty face—lovely eyes, Tom. She's a prize, my boy. (*She closes the magazine and replaces it upon the table.*)—But look out for that chin.

TOM

Why?

DAISY

Just look out for it. (*She goes to him.*)—Does she love you? *Will* she love you, head over heels, regardless, as I—shall I say "as I once did"? Would you rather?

TOM

Daisy—don't—

DAISY

I hold you dear, Tom—*you*—for what you are—just *as* you are. I thought it was my special gift. But maybe she has it too. I hope, I hope—

[*He gropes for her hand, raises it to his lips kisses it.*

TOM

There's no one like you—never will be. *I* know that.— But this—it's the damndest thing—I can't tell you—

DAISY

Don't try.—I'll pray for you every night, Tom. I really shall, you know I do that.

TOM

Oh, my sweet dear——

DAISY

Yes—be good enough to remember me kindly, if you will.

[*She returns to the table.*

TOM (*wretchedly*)

Oh, don't *talk* that stuff!

[*He goes to the fire place. She takes up her work-board.*

DAISY

Now just stand like that a minute, will you? Erect!— Will you stand erect, please?

[*He turns. She looks at him keenly.*

TOM

What's all this about "remembering"? You sound as if we were——

[*She draws one strong line upon the paper and lets the work-board drop.*

DAISY

There! That's all I want of you, all I shall keep of you. So goodbye, you Tom Collier.

[*He looks at her, puzzled.*

TOM

"Goodbye"?—Until when—?

DAISY (*so lightly*)

Doomsday, my darling.

TOM

Daisy, what *are* you talking about!

DAISY

Just that.

[*He advances to her, takes her shoulders in his hands.*

TOM

Now you listen to me: If you think I'm going to allow two people as important to each other as you and I are, to be separated by any such false, ridiculous notion as this, you're mistaken. Just you try it.

DAISY

Tell me goodbye!

TOM

I'll do nothing of the sort.

DAISY

Yes! You have to.—Sharp, decent, clean—no loose ends between *us* two!

TOM

But it's not decent!—It's soft. It's sentimental. It's the sort of thing you've never had any use for— taught *me* never to.

DAISY

Goodbye!

TOM

I will not say it.

DAISY

Goodbye!

TOM

No.

DAISY

You must!

TOM

You'll never get me to. So give up.

[DAISY *throws back her head and closes her eyes in pain.*

DAISY

Oh, sweet heaven, what a world! *I* could do better by people than this—

TOM

Daisy dear—listen to me—

DAISY

—And I want you to take those things of yours— you hear? I don't want them hanging around the place, not me.—That new maid had a very fine hunch about us, didn't she?—Packed you all up, yes. Second sight—well, she gets the gate for it, the big Swede. [*He stands gazing at her.*

TOM

I don't believe in this. I don't believe in any of it. [*She indicates the bedroom.*

DAISY

—Go in and get them, will you? Fetch, Thomas. It's quite a neat, tidy little bundle. You won't be ashamed of it.—But if it stays around—well, I don't quite see myself crying into an old shirt, do you?—I have work to do, my son—a great deal of it. (*He does not move.*) No? Won't fetch?—Then kindly permit me to—(*She moves toward the bedroom.*)—And then you must say goodbye to me—you will, won't you? You've said it so many times, so brightly—Say it this time sadly.—We'll make it an *un*-marriage ceremony, to keep it all quite regular. You must grasp my hand in yours—one splendid gesture—and murmur "Goodbye, my Daisy. Thanks very much. A charming association." (*She goes into the bedroom.*) —And may we never, never meet again so long as we two shall live.—You will, won't you?

[*He has been staring fixedly after her. Suddenly he straightens.*

TOM

—No.

[*He moves swiftly to the hall doorway, picks up his hat and goes out. A moment. Then* DAISY *comes in again, with a small bundle tied up in a large white handkerchief.*

DAISY

—See?—The wash is back.—Now do as Daisy says, and say—

[*She sees that he has gone. She moves toward the*

door, stops against the work-table. The bundle droops in her hand, drops upon the table. There she stands, staring at the door. Again, FRANC's *violin is heard, playing the scales.*

CURTAIN

ACT TWO

ACT TWO

At TOM COLLIER'S. *About half-past seven on a Satur-
day night the following January.*

*The living-room has undergone a certain change.
Small, feminine touches, such as new lamps, cretonne
curtains at the windows and slip-covers of the same
material on chairs and sofa, have made a woman's room
of it.*

CECELIA *and* GRACE MACOMBER *are seated near the
fire place having after-dinner coffee.* GRACE *is just over
thirty. Without a single feature to remark upon except
a slim and well-kept body, she manages, with the aid of
coiffeurs, dressmakers and manicurists, to impress one
as an attractive woman. She puts down her coffee-cup
and moves closer to the fire.*

GRACE

My dear, I'm congealed. I can't say I envy you the
trip into town.

CECELIA

It's not my idea.

[*She takes up a piece* of *needlepoint and begins to
work upon it.*

GRACE

But why do you do it? It's so grim.

63

CECELIA

Tom wants to.

GRACE

Such devotion.

CECELIA

It's her first big concert and he thinks for some reason we ought to be there.

GRACE

Who is she, anyway?

CECELIA

Schmidt, her name is.

[GRACE *laughs.*

GRACE

My dear! Not really!

CECELIA

Franc Schmidt, at that.—Tom says she's supreme.

GRACE

Oh—she's a friend, then.

CECELIA

She used to be.

GRACE (*with meaning*)

I see.

[CECELIA *smiles.*

CECELIA

No, Grace. I doubt if you do.

GRACE

I suppose publishers have to hobnob with all sorts of queer people.

CECELIA

We see very few people of any description any more.

GRACE

Don't tell me about the hermit life you live! I think the least you could do would be to come to my Sunday breakfasts now and then. Tomorrow's will be such fun. Do, C.

CECELIA

Perhaps we shall.

GRACE

—Not if you go in tonight.

CECELIA

Perhaps we shan't go in.

GRACE (*knowingly*)

Ah-ha! (*She looks about her.*)—You know, you could do so much with this house.

CECELIA

—If we weren't so poor.

GRACE

Don't be funny. Your name's Collier, isn't it?

CECELIA

Somehow that doesn't seem to make the difference it might.

GRACE

Well, I think it's brutal the way old Rufus K. hangs onto it.

CECELIA

We seem to manage somehow.

GRACE

I'd take *knives*, my dear, and gouge it out. (*A moment. Then*)—What would he be doing now, for instance? Tom, I mean.

CECELIA

Didn't he say he had letters to write?

[GRACE *seats herself again.*

GRACE

He's really extraordinary. He defeats me.

[CECELIA *laughs.*

CECELIA

What's so extraordinary about writing letters?

GRACE

The minute dinner's finished? Before coffee, even?— I guess I'm just not familiar with publishers' eccentricities.

[*Again* CECELIA *laughs.*

CECELIA

He's a little worried tonight, poor dear.—Some more coffee?—(*She gives* GRACE *a second cup.*)—He has a rather difficult ordeal to face.

GRACE

The concert?

CECELIA

No. Discharging Regan.

GRACE

Reg—?

CECELIA

—When, as and if he gets back from his weekly bat in town.

GRACE

You mean that desperate butler? Oh my dear, I'm so glad! He must have embarrassed you to death,— But how did you manage to persuade Tom to let him go?

CECELIA

I had nothing to do with it.

GRACE

No? (*She laughs gaily.*) I believe that! (TOM *comes in from the other room, with two or three magazines, which he is unwrapping.*) Ah! With us again.

TOM

With you again. (*He looks at his watch.*) Look here, C—hadn't we better be getting under way?

CECELIA

We've got hours. Let's not sit and wait in a stuffy theater.

[*A silence. Then:*

GRACE (*brightly*)

I read the new book you published last week, Tom.

TOM (*without interest*)

Yes? What did you think of it?

GRACE

Superlative, my dear. I was simply ravished!

TOM

Well, that's something, isn't it?

[GRACE *laughs.*

GRACE

—Isn't he beyond words? (*To* TOM.) You're the world's funniest man. You couldn't possibly be funnier.

TOM

You don't know me.

GRACE

Oh yes I do! Don't *you* adore it, C? The book, I mean—

CECELIA

I like it very much. (*She glances at* TOM.) In fact I'm afraid it was I who made Tom do it.

TOM

And I'm afraid I still think it's the worst tripe The Bantam ever published.

GRACE

—But my dear! Everyone's simply devouring it!

TOM

There'll be a lot of sickness this winter.

CECELIA

You're so foolish about it, Tom. (*To* GRACE.)—He'll make enough on that one book to bring out ten he really cares for.

[TOM *unwraps a second magazine.*

TOM

I suppose that's the way it works.

CECELIA

Of course it is. It's simply common sense.

TOM

I suppose so.

CECELIA

Besides, I don't *care* what you say, it *really* is amusing.

TOM

It's tripe.

GRACE

Isn't there such a thing as having too high a standard?

TOM

No, there's not.

[*She looks at him, startled.*

CECELIA

What Grace means—

TOM (*more emphatically still*)

No, C. There is not.

CECELIA

All right, darling. (*He looks over one of the maga-zines. A moment. Then.*) Oh—I meant to tell you: your father wants us to dine with him Wednesday, and spend the night.
[*Grace pricks up her ears.*

TOM

Get us out of it, won't you?

CECELIA

Again? How can I?

TOM

Oh, say I'm up to my ears in work, or something else he won't believe. Say the old boat is frozen stiff.

GRACE

I could easily send you in, in the closed car. Sammy and I might even join you.

TOM

Thanks. We cannot accept your sacrifice.

GRACE

But this weather—in that *racer*! It couldn't be more sobbing.

TOM

Oh yes it could!
[GRACE *rises.*

GRACE

Well, I guess I'd better be "barging along," as they say. I'm sure it's getting colder by the minute.

TOM

Yes—I think we'd best bring the brass monkeys in tonight.

[*He returns to his magazine.*

GRACE

The—? Oh, by the way, do you happen to know a stage-director named Prentice Frith?

TOM

You know, I'm awfully afraid I don't?

GRACE

He's supposed to be the absolute top in amateur dramatics.

TOM

I *can't* imagine how I've missed him.

GRACE

He's coming out especially for my Sunday breakfast tomorrow—

TOM

That's perfectly fine. That's just what Sunday breakfast needs, isn't it?—Of course the coffee must be very hot, as well.

[GRACE *stares.* CECELIA *rises quickly. Finally* GRACE *turns to her.*

GRACE

Good-night, C.

CECELIA

Good-night, Grace. Must you really?

GRACE (*moving toward the hall door.*)

Yes. I'm afraid I must.

[*She goes out, followed by* CECELIA. TOM *lights a cigarette, seats himself upon the stairs and continues to glance through the magazine. A door is heard to close in the hall. A moment, then* REGAN *comes in and makes his way quietly, but only fairly steadily, toward the dining-room door. He has almost reached it, when* TOM *turns.*

TOM

Hi, Red.

REGAN

'Evening.

TOM

Did you have a good day in town?

REGAN

Fine, thanks.

TOM

Lots of beer?

REGAN

No.

TOM

No?

REGAN

—Ale.

TOM

Why ale?

REGAN

It's quicker.

TOM

It's bitter.

REGAN

It's bitter and quicker.

TOM

You don't seem to be in very good shape.

REGAN

I'm in awful shape.

TOM

You'd better get to bed.

REGAN

—Just where I'm headed.
[*He moves toward the door again.*

TOM

—See here a minute first, Red—
[*He turns.* TOM *goes to him and confronts him sternly.*

REGAN

Yes?
[TOM *hesitates. Then.*

TOM

The fact is, that—(*He stops, and concludes.*)
—Bring a couple of bottles of beer, will you?

REGAN

Right.

[*He goes out.* TOM *draws a deep breath of smoke, sinks down upon the sofa, and exhales it slowly.* CECELIA *comes in from the hall.*

CECELIA

You ought to be ashamed, Tom.

TOM

Why?

CECELIA

You were terrible to Grace.

TOM

Why we should be exposed to a woman like that at all, is more than I can make out.

CECELIA

She's perfectly kind and friendly.

TOM

She's a silly, idle, empty, destructive woman. And the woods are full of her.

CECELIA

Grace destructive?—She doesn't know enough to be.

TOM

It's pure instinct with her. If she were malicious, that might be interesting.—Come on—it's nearly eight.

CECELIA

She thought you were trying to insult her.

TOM

Do you have to change or are you ready?

CECELIA

It seemed to *me* you were unnecessarily rude.—I have to change.

TOM (*rising*)

I'll warm up the car.

CECELIA

Now we've simply got to go to her breakfast in the morning.

TOM

Not me.

CECELIA

But you'll have to make *some* gesture toward her.

TOM

I only know one.

CECELIA

Tom—please be serious.

TOM

Darling, I've spent my life trying to get away from her kind of people.

CECELIA

Just what do you call her kind?

TOM

Well—people utterly without stature, without nobility of any sort.

CECELIA

It takes all kinds to make a world, doesn't it?

TOM

Yes—and then what have you got? (*He laughs, takes her face between his hands, and kisses her.*) Go get dressed.

CECELIA

All the same, I insist that if—. What did you say to Regan?

TOM

Why, I—(*He stops and smiles.*)—I told him to bring some beer, but I expect he's forgotten it.

CECELIA

Oh, I see.

TOM

—Anyhow, I've been thinking: He never drinks on duty. Why shouldn't he have a right to get slightly mellow on his one day off?

CECELIA

"Slightly mellow"!—When he came back last week, he could hardly stand. When I said "Good evening" to him he didn't even answer.

TOM

Maybe he couldn't speak.

CECELIA

Probably not.—I said "Don't forget the furnace, Regan," and all he did was to bow like this, with a foolish grin—so low he nearly toppled over.

TOM

It's pretty hard to gauge a bow under those conditions.

CECELIA

Of course *I* think it's selfish of us to keep him.

TOM

Selfish?

CECELIA

We're certainly depriving him of any chance he ever had to make anything of himself.

TOM

But hang it, C—he broke his hand. He'll never fight again.

CECELIA

I don't mean fighting.

TOM

These are hard times: I don't know what else there is for him.

[CECELIA *shrugs and rises.*

CECELIA

All right. Do as you like about him. I'll leave it to you.

TOM

—And anyhow, I feel for some reason that Red's good luck for me. He's—I don't know—we understand each other. I'm awfully fond of him.

CECELIA

You must be, to ruin whatever chance in life he might have.

[*A moment. Then:*

TOM

I wouldn't do that, C. You know I wouldn't.

CECELIA

You're doing it, though. What possibly could be more degrading to a man than housework?

TOM

You're making a regular Simon Legree of me. Where's my whip?

CECELIA

No, it's simply that in your delightful, casual way, you've never thought of his side of it.

TOM (*thoughtfully*)

—I wouldn't do that to Red. I really wouldn't. (*A moment. Then:*) Ring for him, will you?

CECELIA

Not me. I have nothing to do with it.

[TOM *stares in front of him for a moment, then goes to a bell in the wall, presses it and returns to the fire place.*

TOM

I don't know how I'll tell him.

[*A silence. He ponders it. Then:*

CECELIA

I suppose you feel we *really* must go into town to-night—

TOM

Why, yes. Why?

CECELIA

She'll play again, won't she?

TOM

I hope so—and often. But the first concert's an occasion, you know.

CECELIA

I suppose all your old friends will be there, en masse.

TOM

Without a doubt. (*Then, to himself.*)—All week long I've been trying to tell Red—

CECELIA

—The one you were so fond of—the Daisy something—

TOM

—Daisy Sage.

CECELIA

What's *she* doing now?

TOM

Painting, I believe.

CECELIA

Well?

TOM

I don't know. But I should imagine so.—I haven't seen her.

CECELIA

Don't you see any of them anymore?

TOM

No.

CECELIA

But why not, dearest?

[*A moment. Then:*

TOM

They won't see me.

CECELIA

—Won't see *you!*

TOM

No.—Go on now, please, like a good girl, and get ready. (*She turns, passing her hand over her eyes, and moves toward the stairs.*) What's the matter?

CECELIA

Nothing.

TOM

But dear—what is it?

CECELIA

Just this blasted headache, that's all. I've had it all day.

TOM

What a shame.—The cold air will fix you up.

CECELIA

It's that that gave it to me. I'm—honestly, Tom,
I don't think I can face it. Why not telegraph, in-
stead? Best wishes, and all that.

TOM

It wouldn't do.

CECELIA

I'm sure she'd be every bit as glad to have a tele-
gram.

TOM

You don't understand, C. Franc has been working
for years for this. She—(REGAN *comes in with bottles* of *beer and two glasses on a tray.*)—Just put
them there, will you? (*He does so, and turns to go.*)
—And wait a minute. What's the rush? Stick around.

REGAN

Certainly.

[*He waits, steadying himself in the doorway.* TOM
turns again to CECELIA.

TOM

—Sorry, darling, a telegram wouldn't do. I've got
to be there. But there's no particular reason why you
should come. I can go alone.

CECELIA

I'll come.

TOM

No, you hop into bed with a flock of aspirin. I'll be
out again bright and early.

CECELIA

—I'll come, too.

[*She goes out, up the stairs.* TOM *waits a moment, then turns to* REGAN.

TOM

—Drag up a chair.

[REGAN *brings a chair to the table.*

REGAN

One more's about all I need. (TOM *opens the beer and fills the glasses.*) This morning if all the bad heads in the world'd been put together in a row, my head would've got up and sneered at the rest of them.

[TOM *laughs and raises his glass.*

TOM

Here's how.

[REGAN *raises his.*

REGAN

How. (*He drinks, and beams.*) That's the stuff.

TOM

It builds you up.

REGAN

Yo! (*He takes an old pack of cards from his pocket.*) —Seen this one?

TOM

I don't think so.

[REGAN *holds the pack up before him and releases one card after another with his thumb.*

REGAN

—Tell me where to stop, and remember the card.

TOM

All right.

REGAN

Got it?

TOM

I've got it.

[REGAN *makes a concealed "pass," shuffles the pack rapidly and hands it to him.*

REGAN

Where is it?

[TOM *looks through the pack.*

TOM

Gone, of course.

REGAN

Feel in your pocket.

[TOM *feels in his breast-pocket.*

TOM

Not this time.

REGAN

No? (*He reaches into the pocket, draws out a card and shows it to him.*) That it?

TOM

Marvellous.

[REGAN *gloomily returns the pack to his pocket.*

REGAN

I paid five dollars for that one. I'll let it go for two ninety-eight.

TOM

Not interested. (*A moment.*)—Was it cold in town, today?

REGAN

—I don't envy those guys selling apples on the corners.

TOM (*soberly*)

No.—Not much of a job, that.

REGAN

Women's work.

TOM

Pretty tough times, all right.

REGAN

—Some of 'em, by God, are down to selling those white flowers that stink so. (*Again he raises his glass.*) Two hundred for steel!
[*They drink.*

TOM

I'm feeling the pinch a bit myself.

REGAN

—Say, look here, Tom—

TOM

What?

REGAN

If I—(*But he thinks better of it and concludes.*)
—nothing.
[*They finish their glasses.* TOM *refills them.*

TOM (*suddenly*)
Red, I might as well tell you straight off—

REGAN

What?

TOM (*after a moment*)
—Nothing.
[*They drink.*

REGAN

—All goes to show you ought to put something by.

TOM

It certainly does.

REGAN

—Clean up while you're young and close your mitts
on it.

TOM

That's it.
[*A silence. Then:*

REGAN

How's your father these days?

TOM

Never better.
[REGAN *shakes his head.*

REGAN

Tsch-tsch-tsch.

TOM

Red, do you ever think of your future?

REGAN (*ruefully*)

I guess I'll go to hell, all right. (TOM *laughs.*) Oh—
you mean here.—Now that's a funny thing, because
listen, Tom—

TOM

What?

REGAN

I've been thinking: maybe I—(*He falters, and cannot go on.*)—Oh, what the hell—

TOM

But what?

[REGAN *holds out his glass.*

REGAN

Fill her up, will you?

[TOM *refills both glasses.*

TOM

Not much future in buttling, eh, Red?

REGAN (*with a deprecatory gesture*)

Oh, well—

TOM

I'm—I'm certainly very grateful for all you've done.

REGAN (*uncomfortably*)

Ah!—Be still, will you?

TOM

I am, though.

REGAN

That's fine, from you.—I'll never forget, when I was
—and you—(*He gulps.*) I'll never forget it.
[*He sniffs, and drinks.*

TOM

Put it there, old man. (*They clasp hands across the
table.*) You're a fine fellow.

REGAN

You're the top, boy. I don't know what you'll think
of me, when I—
[*Again, he is unable to continue.*

TOM

When you what?

REGAN

When I—well, what would you say, for instance, if
I—(*He looks at him, then looks away.*) Nope, it's no
good—

TOM (*anxiously*)

You're not in trouble, are you?

REGAN

Trouble? Me? What trouble?
[TOM *once more refills the glasses. Then, steeling
himself:*

TOM

—Then look here, Regan—

REGAN

Well, Chief?

[TOM *looks at him. The steel melts.*

TOM

—Good old Red.

[REGAN *raises his glass.*

REGAN

Tom Collier for President. The People's Choice.

TOM

Listen a minute—

REGAN

Wait! (*He takes another deep draught.*)Tom, I've just got to tell you. I've—I've—(*He grasps for* TOM's *hand and misses it.*)—Don't hold it against me, Tom, but I'm quitting you. I've took another job.

[TOM *half-rises in astonishment.*

TOM

You've—?!

REGAN

Oh, I know what you'll say!

[TOM *drops into his chair again, and stares.*

TOM

Holy cats, Red—

REGAN

I couldn't stand it any longer. She don't like my

ways. I mean the Missus. I get on her nerves.—Last
week Moe Winters told me he wanted to open a country gym and would I run it with him, on the order of
Muldoon's, but with a little bar attached and, well,
God help me, I give him my word.

TOM

What's there in it for you?

REGAN

Don't put it that way, Tom.

TOM

But I really want to know.

REGAN

Two hundred a month, and a smell at the gate, if
any.

TOM

It sounds like a good deal.

REGAN

Ah, the hell with it!—Let's let it go. I'll phone him.

TOM (*alarmed*)

No! (REGAN *looks at him.*) When do you start?

REGAN

He wanted me last Wednesday. I've been trying all
week to get up the nerve to tell you. But—

TOM

How long will it take you to pack?

[REGAN *grins.*

REGAN

Well, there's my hat-trunk and my shoe-trunk, and the trunk for my fancy-dress ball-clothes—

TOM (*firmly*)

You leave by noon tomorrow, you hear? Not a minute later.

[REGAN's *grin fades.*

REGAN

O.K., Chief.—I'm sorry you had to take it this way.

TOM

Don't be a fool. I'm overjoyed for you.

REGAN (*uncertainly*)

Fact?

TOM

Absolute. (*He raises his glass.*) Here's to the new job.

REGAN

—Take it from me, boy, you're the goods.

TOM

You've got your points, too, you know.

[REGAN *rises, swaying slightly, and raises his glass.*

REGAN

Anyhow—

[TOM *rises and raises his.*

TOM

Anyhow.

[*They drain their glasses, put them down and again clasp hands.*

REGAN

You'll explain to the Missus?

TOM

Of course.

REGAN

Tell her I'm sorry—hope no inconvenience—but—

TOM

I'll explain.

REGAN

So long, Tom.

TOM

Good-bye, Red.

REGAN

So long, Tom.

TOM

Good-bye, Red.

REGAN

I'll give you a ring how it goes.

TOM

Do that.

REGAN

Keep your bib clean.

TOM

I will, old boy.

[*Suddenly* REGAN *sobers, looks at him intently for a long moment, then touches him on the shoulder and says:*

REGAN

Good luck, Tom.

[*Turns abruptly, and swiftly and steadily goes to the door and out.* TOM *takes a deep breath and seats himself at the table, with his back to the stairs, in utter dejection. He picks up* REGAN's *pack of cards and moodily glances through it.* CECELIA *comes down the stairs in a lovely negligee. A moment, then she speaks lowly.*

CECELIA

Tom——

TOM (*without turning*)

Hello. Ready?

CECELIA

Did you tell him?

TOM

I'll miss that guy. I'll miss having him around.
[*She goes to him.*

CECELIA

I know, dear. But it's for the best. I'm sure of it.
[TOM *puts down the cards.*

TOM

I've got a feeling that my luck's going with him.

CECELIA

No, no!—I'm your luck.

[*She draws him into her arms and takes his head against her breast. A moment. Then:*

TOM

You feel good, C.

CECELIA

Do I, dear?

TOM

You haven't any clothes on. Go on—dress—dress quickly—we've got to run.

[*She moves from him toward the stairs, where she turns again.*

CECELIA

—Come and help me? (*He looks at her for an instant, then goes to her. She turns into his arms. He holds her to him for a moment, then she leans away from him, provocatively.*) No, you'd better not. (*She glances down at the negligee, arms out.*) Look—I came across it in the bottom drawer, and my spine simply melted.—Do you remember it?

[*He picks up the edge of the loose sleeve and kisses it.*

TOM

—Quebec.

CECELIA

Then you do!—That funny little French hotel—

TOM (*gazing at her*)

Yes.

CECELIA

—Darling place.—Wasn't it cold that morning?—
Frost on the windows an inch thick.—Remember?

TOM

—We couldn't see out—

CECELIA

We didn't want to.

TOM

No one else could see in.

CECELIA

Breakfast before the fire—shivering.—Remember—?

TOM

I remember.

CECELIA

We didn't finish it—

TOM

No.

CECELIA (*with a little laugh*)

There was only one way to keep warm.
[*He moves toward her.*

TOM

Oh C, darling—
[*She retreats, up one step of the stairs.*

CECELIA

No.—You'll make us late.

TOM

What of it?

CECELIA

It's late already. It's—we might miss the concert altogether.

TOM

What if we do?

CECELIA

Tom, you're the limit! Ten minutes ago you said—. (*A moment. Then, in another voice.*) Tom—

TOM

Oh yes, darling. What—

CECELIA

You go in alone. I've decided to stay here.

TOM

You've—?

CECELIA

Yes. It's too cold. I'm going to tuck myself into my warm bed, and—you'll need your heavy coat, won't you? It's here—(*She goes into the hall, returning with an overcoat which she leaves upon a chair.*) Good-night, love. I'll miss you—(*He is about to take her in his arms, but she retreats, with the same provocative smile and an admonitory gesture.*) No, no!—Good-night, dear. Keep warm.

[*He turns from her. She mounts the stairs, turns once, smiles down upon him curiously, and goes out leaving the door open. A moment. Then he takes up his coat, crosses the room, puts out the lights, and is returning to the hall doorway, when he hears CE-CELIA singing lowly to herself from upstairs. He stops, listens a moment, then moves slowly to the side table, where he leaves his coat upon a chair and takes up the telephone.*

TOM

Western Union, please. (*A moment.*) Western Union? (*The curtain begins to fall.*) I want to send a tele-gram.

CURTAIN

ACT TWO

SCENE II

At DAISY SAGE'S. *Late afternoon on a fine bright day the following May. The sitting-room is as before, except for the painting-materials upon the work-table, and a large easel, turned away from the front, at the window.*

JOE *is seated upon the sofa, smoking.* FRANC *stands at the window, looking out. A moment, then she turns abruptly to* JOE.

FRANC

—But what if *she* doesn't come?

JOE

She'll come.

[FRANC *leaves the window and seats herself, tense, upon a chair near him.*

FRANC

My nerves are like that.

JOE

Have a cigarette?

FRANC

No.

JOE

It ought to be quite a meeting. Only that once, months ago—think of it.

FRANC

And in a speakeasy!

JOE

—Like old times, though, like a reunion. That is, until *they* came for him.—You know, I think the last thing he wanted to do was to go on to that party with them.

FRANC

She is a pretty, the wife.—But did you notice? In his top hat, when he put it on, suddenly he looked like only anybody.

JOE

Domestication works fast, when it works.

FRANC

—Well, Daisy has not spoke of him one time since. Never, never will she forgive us this.—Give me a cigarette. What did he say to you?

[*He gives her a cigarette and lights it for her.*

JOE

He just telephoned that he wanted to see me, said it seemed years.—Your hand's shaking.

FRANC

I know it.—What did you tell him?—Why shouldn't it shake?

JOE

I said I'd be back at five. Then I left a note on the door: "Had to go to Daisy's. Come there."—It wouldn't if you smoked less.

FRANC

At five. (*She looks at her watch.*) Ach, Gott!

JOE

You're getting emotional in your old age, Frankie.

FRANC

—But why did you do it? It was well enough left alone.

JOE

I like Tom, and he sounded pathetic. I imagine he saw her exhibition, and—

FRANC

What makes you think he did?

JOE

He said he was telephoning from the Overton Gallery.—I wonder what he thought of it.

FRANC

What did you?

JOE

I know so damn little about painting.

FRANC

I know less.—But it all seemed to me so fresh—done with such spirit.

JOE

That's it!

FRANC

—Bold—what-you-call it—un—in—without compromising.

JOE

Yes.—And the real stuff. No fakiness.

FRANC

—Every one of them Daisy. No little Matisses or Picassos.
[*A moment.*

JOE

But Franc—

FRANC (*nerves again*)
Yes? All *right*. What?

JOE

What really did you think of them?
[*She shrugs.*

FRANC

I tell you I am not—what-you-say—competent to judge.

JOE

What did they do to you, Franc?
[*She looks at him sharply, hesitates. Then:*

FRANC

—Nothing. I am sorry. But nothing—

JOE

Nor to me.

[*She grasps his arm.*

FRANC

—But we must believe in her, Joe!

JOE (*in pain*)

We do, don't we?—Oh Lord, if only all my friends made shirts for a living.

FRANC

Yes. You could say "That is not a good shirt" quite easily.

JOE

This afternoon—after a few minutes we duck out on them, understand?

FRANC

Joe, I don't like it. I am afraid of this. I think it is not wise.

JOE

—If only they'd have one of their good old-time rows. I'll bet he and that wife of his never had a decent scrap in their lives.

FRANC (*thoughtfully*)

—And still, maybe seeing him, Daisy finds it is all over—finished—cold. Sometimes that is so. I hope for her it will be so.

JOE

Listen, child: it's May, and the trees are in bloom.

FRANC (*scornfully*)

You should write in German.

JOE

Poor Tom. Poor guy. He's up against it for fair now, Franc.

FRANC

Why now more than usual?

JOE

Well, I ran into Hal Foster today, and—

FRANC

Foster—?—The one who did those stories?

JOE

That's the boy. He's finished a new novel that's even better, they say. Apparently Tom thinks he can grab it for The Bantam, and stage a comeback on the strength of it. A sort of a last straw. He's to meet him this afternoon.

FRANC

Oh, good!

[JOE *shakes his head.*

JOE

No, not so: Foster told me that hard up as he is, he'd be damned before he'd go with a house that was responsible for "Young Ecstasy" and—

FRANC

But you should have talked to him, Joe!

JOE

I did, till I was blue in the face. He just kept saying "Then how about *you?*" It was no use explaining how Tom thought I'd do better with—(JOE *glances quickly at the door, and rises.*) Look out!

FRANC

Him?

JOE

Yes, or—(DAISY *comes in.*) Oh, hello, Daisy!

[DAISY *pulls off her hat and gloves and looks at them.*

DAISY

My, you're hearty. (*To* FRANC.) What's the matter?

FRANC

With me?

DAISY

Yes. You look queer.

FRANC

I don't like the Spring. I don't like May and the trees in bloom.

DAISY

No? Nor do I. I say it's maple-syrup, and I say the hell with it. (*She seats herself near them.*) Well, the show's over. It's been a fine week. I've learned a lot about new painters, the so-called Public and the so-called Press.

FRANC

There are no judges of one's work but oneself, Daisy.

DAISY

Then you don't by any chance agree with them?

FRANC

I would sooner sleep with an art critic than agree with him.

DAISY

It's touching the way my friends have rallied round. Stout hearts. Thanks, thanks.—But oh heaven!— If only someone I love and trust would be honest with me!

JOE

And what do you *call* what we've been?

DAISY

Friendly, Joe, very friendly.

JOE

I tell you: let's all get drunk.

DAISY

No thanks. (*For a brief moment she covers her face with her hands, then looks up again.*) It's all right. It's over. Let's talk about something. Who knows anything?

[*A silence.* DAISY's *head sinks again. Finally* FRANC *ventures:*

FRANC

Jim and Nancy Peters are going to have a baby.

DAISY (*absently*)

A boy?

FRANC

I think so.

DAISY

Good for them.
[*Another silence. Then:*

JOE

—Er—Tom Collier rang me up this afternoon.
[*A moment. Then:*

DAISY

Oh? How is he?

JOE

He sounded sunk.

DAISY

That's too bad. (*She cools her wrists. Then, to* FRANC.)—You know, it's *hot.*

FRANC

It *is* hot.—Don't be bitter, Daisy.

DAISY

I heard grand things about Nova Scotia yesterday.— Why should I be bitter?

FRANC

You shouldn't.—About what? Where is it?

DAISY

North, way north.—Bitter! Me!—They say it's beautiful beyond words, and you can live there on oh, so little.

JOE

He said—I mean Tom did—that—

DAISY

Joe, you seem to have an idea that I might be interested in what he'd say—

JOE

Well—

DAISY

But as it happens, I'm not. (*To* FRANC.) There are miles of green meadows and a seacoast that's nobody's business. Woods, as well. (*To* JOE.)—I suppose he was full of explanations about those choice eggs The Bantam Press has been laying lately.

JOE

No, he didn't mention them. He only said—

DAISY

Why tell *me*? (*To* FRANC.) The only out's the swimming. It's too cold. But other things make up for it. (*To* JOE.)—He always gets colds in the Spring— I suppose his voice was gone entirely—

JOE

It didn't seem to be.

DAISY (*to* FRANC)

It's like Maine, they say. Only better, much.

FRANC

Not too many people?

[DAISY *closes her eyes.*

DAISY

No people. Gloriously, happily, mercifully, no people. (*The buzzer at the door sounds.*) Joe—will you?
(*To* FRANC.)—Speaking of no people. (JOE *presses a
button to open the door.* DAISY *continues to* FRANC.)
Imagine Joe thinking that at this date *I* should give
a damn what—

[TOM *comes in with a brief-case in his hand.*

TOM

Joey! How are you? (*He drops the brief-case upon
the work-table.*) Franc!

FRANC

Tom, you look fine.

[*He turns to* DAISY.

TOM

Hello, Daisy.

DAISY (*so coolly*)

Hello. How have you been?

TOM

In rude health, thanks.—And you?

DAISY

Never better.

TOM

Oh, it's fine to see you! I've been starving for you—
all of you.

DAISY

Thanks.

TOM

How's the job?

DAISY

The magazine job?

TOM

Yes.

DAISY

I gave it up last winter.—A trifle—shall we say "quixotic"?—of me?

TOM

Shall we? (*He looks from one to the other of them.*) Listen: I love you three, I love you. (*He takes* FRANC's *head in his hands and kisses her brow.*) Oh Lord! (*Gives* JOE *a friendly shove.*) Lord Almighty— (*Laughs joyfully, seats himself and gazes fondly at them. There is a long silence. Finally:*) Holy cats! Talk to me, will you?—Am I a leper? (*Silence. He leans forward.*) Now listen, the lot of you: I've had enough of this nonsense. For months you've been avoiding me like the plague and I won't stand for it. You're important to me and by heaven, I'm going to hang onto your coat-tails, dog your footsteps, sit on your doorsteps, until you're ready to grant that a man can marry, and go on being a friend.—Is that understood?—Well, then: who's seen Sandy Patch? [*Then, in a rush:*

JOE

I have.

FRANC

So have I.

DAISY

We all have.

TOM

What's he doing?

JOE

A war group in bronze for some town in Texas. He's making them look like sheep.

TOM

Good boy!

DAISY

—Except that they'll probably throw it back at him.

JOE

He'll get paid, though. Sam Frankl sees to that for him now.

TOM

How's your book doing?

JOE

Fair.—Of course nothing like The Bantam's "Indian Summer" or "Young Ecstasy."

TOM

Ouch.

JOE

What the devil made you take them on?

TOM

Money.—Ah, but Joey, I'm reforming! Did you know it?

JOE

In time, I hope.— How?

TOM

Williamson, Warren can have those bright boys now, and welcome.

JOE

It's about where they belong.

TOM

Wait till you see The Bantam's new list.

JOE

I'm waiting.

TOM

—That was certainly a foul format Brandon gave your book.

JOE

The words are there.

TOM

If you can read them. What's the stock they printed it on—paper-towelling?—I hear you're a hit, Franc.

FRANC

It has gone well enough.

[*He looks at* DAISY, *hesitates. Then:*

TOM

I—I saw your exhibition today.

DAISY

Oh really?—Funny I missed you. What did you think of it?

TOM

Well—

DAISY (*suddenly, eagerly*)

Tell me!

TOM

I don't think you were ready to show yet. How did it happen?

DAISY

Saunders and Munn arranged it.

TOM

Your old editors? The fashion boys?

DAISY

What about it?

[TOM *shakes his head.*

TOM

Daisy, Daisy.—How were the notices?

DAISY

Appalling.

TOM

I suppose their reasons were all wrong—

DAISY

Of course.—What are yours?

[*A moment. Then:*

TOM

Well, you've been painting less than a year—

DAISY

Yes.

TOM

—And yet you had about thirty canvases to show.
[*Now* DAISY *is well on her mettle.*

DAISY

Thirty-two.

TOM

It's a lot, Daisy.

DAISY

So you didn't care for any of them.

TOM

Oh yes!—One I loved particularly: the one of the
doorstep, with the milk-bottles. I'd like to own that
one.

DAISY

—Number Seven.—Sorry, it's not for sale.

TOM

Two hundred—?

DAISY

Nope.

TOM

Two-fifty!

DAISY

Nope.

TOM

Seventy-five—

DAISY

Nope.

TOM

Four hundred and one—

DAISY

Nope.

TOM

I wouldn't take it as a gift.

DAISY

That's all right, then.

TOM

Of course your drawing's a marvel. Lord, how that's come along!

DAISY

—Only what?

TOM

Good draughtsmanship's not to be sneezed at, is it?

DAISY

Certainly not. Look at Belcher.

TOM

No—at Goya.

DAISY

Thanks so much.

TOM

Of course it depends on what you want to be. I thought it was a painter.

[FRANC *rises.*

DAISY

So did I.—Goya painted pretty well, too, I thought.

TOM

In the first year? I doubt it.

DAISY

I wasn't aware it took a definite length of time.

TOM

—And living in cities all your life, you know.

DAISY

Perhaps I'd better hie me to some sylvan dell.

TOM

I don't think it would hurt a bit.

DAISY

—Listen, you: if you can show me a purer cobalt than the winter sky over the East River any afternoon at four—

TOM

That's not the point.

[DAISY's *voice is higher.*

DAISY

What is?

TOM

Fever—rush—hysteria—all day, every day.

[DAISY *turns away.*

DAISY

Oh, go to hell, will you?

[FRANC *moves toward the door.*

TOM

Sure. When do we start?

FRANC

Come along, Joe.

[JOE *follows her.*

DAISY

—And leave me with this mossback? This—(*Again she turns upon* TOM.)—So I'm to sit under a parasol and paint tight little cows in streams, am I?

TOM

That's not what I said.

[*Unnoticed by* DAISY, JOE *and* FRANC *have gone out.*

DAISY

—Something suitable as an over-mantel for the Home of Her Dreams, I suppose.

TOM

Now you're being bull-headed.

DAISY (*turning*)

Bull-headed!—He calls *me* bull—(*She sees that* FRANC *and* JOE *are no longer there.*) Oh, you snakes—

TOM (*with a gesture*)

Well—

DAISY

Well? What more, Teacher?

TOM

All I said and all I'm saying is, you can't expect, the first *crack* out of the box, to—*you've* got to *work*, Daisy.

DAISY

Sweet heaven! What else have I been doing? What have I done but?

TOM

—But differently—with such pains. You're turning out too much, you know it.

[*Suddenly the fight goes out of her.*

DAISY

Maybe, maybe.—Anything's too much.

TOM

Ah, darling—

DAISY

No!—Don't soften on me. Stay tough!

TOM

I do believe that's it, though. I believe it's the whole story: still hung over from the old job. Pressure, pressure all the time. Still rushing countless sketches through against a magazine's deadline.

[*She looks away from him. Her hand gropes blindly for his and finds it.*

DAISY

—Anyway, against some deadline—

TOM

Daisy—darling—

DAISY

You're cruel, inhuman. You're a brute.

TOM

Oh Daisy—

DAISY

Thanks for being.

TOM

If you mean it—

DAISY

From my heart—(*She looks at him, smiling now.*)
Oh, you skunk—
[*He laughs, relieved.*

TOM

Worse. Much worse.

DAISY (*serious again*)

Who but you, Tom? (*She points her finger at him.*)
Look: only you and strangers honest with me ever.
[*He draws her down beside him on the sofa.*

TOM

—The country's the place to work, Daisy. Listen:
There's a grand little house about six miles from us.
Woods, hills, meadows—you can get it for almost
nothing.

DAISY

That's about my price.

TOM

It could easily be painted up. What about a white roof for it?

DAISY

Oh, lovely idea!

TOM

C discovered it. She can find out all about it. I'll tell her who it's for.

[*But at this,* DAISY's *mood changes.*

DAISY

Don't dream of it.

TOM

Why not?

DAISY

I've got other places in mind.

TOM

Anyhow, go somewhere.

DAISY

Sure—somewhere.

TOM

You're going to be good, Daisy, Don't think I don't think you're good.

DAISY

I won't. I won't think anything.

TOM

This is a big day for me, do you know it?

DAISY

How?

TOM

Well, I've been seeing the folly of my ways here lately. Poor C—I must have been sweet to live with this past week. She's been grand about it, though.

DAISY

I'm sure she has.

TOM

I—suddenly, for some reason, I saw that I'd got off the track—my track. It was pretty painful— But I'm getting back on, I think.

DAISY

I'm glad, Tom. You must, you know.

TOM

Did you ever hear of a fellow named Hal Foster?

DAISY

No. What does he do?

TOM

Writes. My God, how he writes!—And nobody knows it—not yet—

DAISY

Have you got him?

TOM

I'm getting him. He's done a fine, poisonous short novel that makes Candide look sick. (*In growing excitement.*) I'm going to make a grand type-job of it, advertise it all over the place, and sell it at two bucks. I don't care if I lose my shirt on it.—I'm to meet him at six this afternoon, to make arrangements.

DAISY

It must be nearly that now. You'd better go.

TOM

—Daisy.—Have you missed me, Daisy?

DAISY

You? Well, I'll tell you, it's this way: I—
[*But she stops and looks at him, drops her bantering tone, and nods, dumbly.*

TOM

Much?
[*Again she nods, and adds, under her breath:*

DAISY

—Skunk, skunk.

TOM

Oh, and I you!—It's a lot of nonsense, this. It's ridiculous.
[*She looks at her watch.*

DAISY

It *is* six.

TOM

Hell.

DAISY

You'd better run.

TOM

We need each other, we two do.

DAISY

You think?

TOM

Most terribly. I'm convinced of it. There never were
such friends as you and me. It's wicked to give that
up, to lose anything so fine for no good reason.—
Why you, of all people, for a shabby, lowdown ques-
tion of convention, fit only to be considered by
shabby, lowdown—

DAISY

Wait a minute!

TOM

A hundred times I'd have given my eyes to see you,
to talk to you—

DAISY

Well—here I am—

TOM (*eagerly*)

Daisy—may I come again?—Just now and then, you
know?

DAISY (*after a moment*)

—If you like—just now and then.

TOM

Oh my sweet dear—thanks!

DAISY

But don't say "sweet dear." That belongs to another
life, years ago.

TOM

Oh—there are to be rules, are there?

DAISY

One or two. One strict one—
[*She hesitates.*

TOM

What?

DAISY

Never secret. Never hidden.

TOM

No, no!

DAISY

—Always open, as before.

TOM

But of course, of course!

DAISY

I couldn't go it otherwise.

TOM

Why should a friendship be hidden? What's there
to hide?

DAISY

It gets misunderstood.

TOM

It won't, it can't, or the whole world's rotten.

DAISY

It's been pretty ripe for a long time, Tommy.

TOM

"Tommy"! (*He laughs exultantly and draws her into his arms. They stand rocking back and forth, laughing in delight.*) Oh my darling, how grand this is!

DAISY

I see you run to tweeds this season.

TOM

I even have a horse now—practically a county squire.

DAISY

Look out for it.

TOM

Oh, it's tame.

DAISY

I mean going county.

TOM

Never you fear! I wouldn't be let. I'm a terribly queer duck to them.

DAISY

"Lit'ry," I suppose.

TOM

"Very artistic."

DAISY

Are they good and dull?

TOM

Crashing.

DAISY

—And respectable.

TOM

My God, how!

DAISY

We aren't respectable.

TOM

Not a bit. Never shall be.

DAISY

For which, praise heaven.

TOM

Heaven, I praise you that Daisy and I are not—. Kiss the boy, Daisy.

DAISY

No.—You've got to go.

TOM

Why? Would it take long?

[*She laughs, and pecks his cheek.*

DAISY

There.

TOM

Ask me am I happy—

DAISY

It's all right, isn't it?

TOM

Magnificent.—All as before.

DAISY

Yes.—But for one thing.

TOM

What?

[*She leaves his arms.*

DAISY

We aren't in love any more.—Now run. You might miss what's-his-name.

TOM

How about lunch tomorrow?

DAISY

It's fine with me.

TOM

The old place?

DAISY

I'd love it.

TOM

One o'clock?

DAISY

One o'clock.

TOM

—And we'll dine at John Donovan's. He's opened a new place on Forty-eighth Street.

DAISY

Dine?

TOM

Why not?

DAISY

All right.

TOM

The next day's Wednesday, isn't it? I said I'd drive
out in the morning to see Pat Atkins. He's been sick
again.

DAISY

Poor dear. I'm sorry.

TOM

He's better now.—Come along with me, Daisy.

DAISY

Wednesday? No— Wednesday, I—

TOM

If it's a good day we'll take a picnic. What do you
say?

DAISY

I—I guess so.

TOM

Fine!—We'll get back in time to—let's see, can I
stay in town Wednesday night? Yes, of course, I can.
I want to see that black woman dance.

DAISY

Which one?

TOM

Down on Grand Street.

DAISY

Oh yes, I've heard about her!

TOM

We can look in, anyway.—Thursday I'm at the Press all day. But Friday—

DAISY

Wait a minute, Tom.—You said only now and—.

TOM

I'll bring Hal Foster in about four on Friday. Will you be here?

DAISY

I—I think so.

TOM

Good-bye then, darling. Till tomorrow!

DAISY

Good-bye, Tom.

[*He takes her face in his hands, kisses it several times, then her mouth, briefly:*

TOM

Sweet dear, sweet dear—. (*He releases her.*) One o'clock?

DAISY

One o'clock.

[*He goes swiftly to the door, where he turns once more.*

TOM

—*Ten minutes* to one!

[*He is gone, his footsteps heard upon the stairs. She stands rigid, exalted, her eyes shining. Then she sees his brief-case, left behind him upon the work-table. She stares at it for a long time, apprehension grow-ing in her eyes. Then she murmurs "Franc," runs to the door, flings it open and calls in terror:*

DAISY

Franc!

[*Then returns, puts* TOM'S *brief-case upon a chair, then places a work-box upon her table and begins filling it with tools and materials.* FRANC *comes in.*

FRANC

Daisy?—What is it? Your voice frightened me.

DAISY

Franc, you're the one woman I know who can hold her tongue.

[FRANC *shrugs.*

FRANC

What is not my business— (*She sees what* DAISY *is doing, and her casual air is replaced by a real anx-iety.*) Packing? What's this? What for? You and—? Oh, Daisy, hold on a minute. Wait, Liebchen. Think, are you wise, Daisy—

DAISY

I'm going alone—a long way, for a long time.

FRANC

To that place you said?

DAISY (*a sudden idea*)

Yes!

FRANC

Wait! I come with you—

DAISY

No, I don't want anyone now. Later, maybe.

FRANC

But what is it, dear?

DAISY

I guess I'm running for my life, Franc.

FRANC

—Tom again.

DAISY

—Still.

FRANC

It's no better—

DAISY (*packing furiously*)

—It's worse.

FRANC

Poor child.

DAISY

No, no! I'm glad.—But I've got to get out.

FRANC

Yes, that is wise.

DAISY

No one's to know where I've gone to.

FRANC

No.

DAISY

No mess—it's to avoid one I'm going.

FRANC

—But compose yourself, Daisy. Be calm.

DAISY

I can't! Look— (*She points to the brief-case.*) He went without it. He'll come back for it. And if I see him again for one more minute I'll die.

FRANC

He loves you, Daisy?

DAISY

I don't know. I don't believe *he* knows. But— (*She looks up from her packing.*) Oh Franc—he's so young!—Did you notice how young he looked?

FRANC

Yes, like a child.

DAISY

All slim and brown and sandy.

FRANC

Quick, Daisy!

DAISY (*far away*)

He'll always be like that—even when he's old. I

know!—And the way he stands—that funny way—
stiff—with his feet out—

FRANC

—What they call duck-footed, eh?

DAISY (*indignantly*)

Not at all. It's a perfectly natural way to stand. It's
a fine, strong way to stand.

FRANC

Hurry, darling. Run quick!

DAISY

Yes, yes, I must.

[*She resumes her packing.*

FRANC

Will you take a trunk?

DAISY

The small one.

FRANC

How do you go—by train?

DAISY

I don't know. Boat, I think.

FRANC

But when? From where?

DAISY

I guess Boston. (*A moment.*) Perhaps I'd better see
him just once more. Maybe if I can explain to him
how impossible it is for us to—

FRANC

No!—And you go to Boston tonight.

DAISY

Yes. Yes, that's right. (FRANC *goes into the bedroom.* DAISY *continues to pack for a moment, then calls:*) Franc!

FRANC

What now?

DAISY

When those things come back from the Gallery, cover them, will you?

FRANC

Yes, dear.

DAISY

—Number Seven—do you hear me, Franc?

FRANC

I hear.

DAISY

Pack Number Seven and send it to him at the Press. [FRANC *re-enters.*

FRANC

All right, dear.

DAISY

You're lunching with him tomorrow.

FRANC

So?

DAISY

At the old place, at one o'clock.

FRANC

One o'clock.

DAISY

Franc—

FRANC

Yes, darling?

[DAISY *gathers up some paint-tubes.*

DAISY

When you see him—

FRANC

Yes, darling—

DAISY

Kiss him for me. (*She realizes what she has said, and murmurs:*) Kiss him for me— (*Then hurls a tube into the box, in fury.*) *Kiss* him for me!

[*The buzzer sounds imperatively.* DAISY *starts in alarm.* FRANC *takes her arm.*

FRANC

Come—and don't speak—

[*She leads her toward the bedroom, stopping to press the button at the fire place. They go out.* TOM *is heard running up the stairs. He hurries in, calling:*

TOM

Daisy—? (*There is no answer. He goes to the table, and calls again:*) Daisy!

[*A moment. Then* DAISY's *voice is heard faintly from the next room.*

DAISY

Hello—

TOM

I forgot my case. (*He finds it upon the chair and picks it up.*) It's all right. I've got it. (*At the door he turns once more and calls:*) Don't be late to-morrow! Remember! Twelve-thirty!

[*And goes out. Again footsteps are heard upon the stairs, and a door slams below.*

CURTAIN

ACT THREE

ACT THREE

SCENE I

At TOM COLLIER's, *six months later. Ten o'clock of a bright Sunday morning. Alterations have been made, and the old library has become a chaste dining-room. Now, at last,* TOM's *house is* CECELIA's *house, which is to say, The House in Good Taste.*

The door beside the fire place at Right opens, through the hall, upon a large new living-room. The library furniture has been replaced with a dining-room table, sideboard, serving-table and chairs. The large table is set for breakfast and there are various breakfast dishes being kept hot upon the serving-table.

CECELIA *and* OWEN *are at breakfast,* CECELIA *seated and* OWEN *standing, napkin in hand, half turned in the direction of the serving-table, toward which* GRACE *is moving with a coffee-cup.*

GRACE

Oh no, thanks! I love to serve myself. It's so English.

[OWEN *reseats himself.* GRACE *refills her cup and returns to the table with it.* CECELIA *presses a button upon the table.*

CECELIA

I'll order some more hot.

[OWEN *takes a swallow of water, puts down his napkin and pushes back his chair.*

137

OWEN

Well, for the morning after a party, I feel pretty good. Where's the birthday-boy?

CECELIA

Still recovering upstairs.

GRACE

He was never more amusing. Honestly, when he did that skit from his new magazine, I thought I couldn't stand it. I was in stitches.

OWEN

—What's happened to the artistic element? Still asleep?

CECELIA

Miss Sage and Fisk insisted upon walking to the station with La Schmidt. It turned out that she had to take an early train.

GRACE

I've never known a musician to make such difficulties about playing.

CECELIA

She's used to her own violin.

GRACE

But is there any differ—? (*Then, thoughtfully.*) Yes—I suppose there is.—The Sage is rather a number, isn't she? Do you know she actually spent six months in Tierra del Fuego?

OWEN

Nova Scotia.

GRACE

I mean Nova Scotia.

CECELIA

Yes, I'd heard.

GRACE

The places they go!—C, I wish I knew how you get hold of such interesting people.

CECELIA

I asked them as a particular favor, for Tom's birthday. I insisted on it. It was part of the surprise party.

[GRACE *sighs*.

GRACE

—They invariably *say* they'll come to me, and then at the last minute something always happens.

CECELIA

—Besides they're very old friends of his. I said he was longing to see them.—I think he really has missed them a little.

OWEN

Clever Cecelia.

CECELIA

Why?

OWEN

Real security at last, eh?

CECELIA

Do you object?

[GRACE *looks at them suspiciously.*

GRACE

What are you talking about? (*There is no answer. She rises.*) Oh, you subtle people! I wish I were subtle.

[CECELIA *presses the bell again.*

CECELIA

I wish someone would answer this bell.

[GRACE *looks about her.*

GRACE

Darling, you *have* done wonders with this house. It's all in such perfect taste, now.

CECELIA

I wish Tom was as enthusiastic about it as you are.

GRACE

Oh, men never like changes.

CECELIA

Unless they think of them themselves.—We're having a charming time about the *roof.*

OWEN

The roof?

CECELIA

It's got to be fixed—and ever since he came back from Bermuda last winter he's been saying he wanted a white roof—been wanting to whitewash it white.

GRACE

What!?

OWEN (*simultaneously*)

The roof here?

CECELIA

Yes. They're all white in Bermuda.

OWEN

But this isn't Bermuda.

CECELIA

I've tried to explain that to him.

OWEN (*to* GRACE)

But I don't think I've ever seen a white roof around here, have you?

GRACE

Let me think. (*She thinks, painfully. Then:*)—No.

CECELIA

He says, What does that matter? He wants one. He thinks they're pretty. He thinks— (*In sudden irritation.*) Oh, he can be exasperating! (*To* OWEN.) His father sent him a check for his birthday: he may accept it, he may not.

GRACE

Not accept a *check*?

CECELIA

—Because it's from him.

GRACE

Well, I'm amazed.—A whopper, too, I'll bet.

CECELIA

I don't know. I didn't see it.

OWEN

I thought he'd got over the nonsense about his father.

CECELIA

So did I. Everything has been simply beautiful for months. He's been so pleased with Tom, and the way business has been going. Apparently someone told him about it.

OWEN

Williamson, probably.

CECELIA

—Or Warren. I don't know which.

GRACE

Are they the ones that want to buy The Bantam Press?

CECELIA

—To buy into it, yes.

GRACE

How does Tom feel about that?

[CECELIA *shrugs.*

OWEN

He's made the price so high they'll have to refuse it.

CECELIA

Not if *you* tell them not to, Owen!

OWEN

I thought I'd explained all that to you.

[*A moment. Then:*

CECELIA

—I suppose I'll have to get the coffee myself. (*She rings again.*) I told Tom that with *him* back, the maids would do nothing.

OWEN

It does seem funny, seeing him around again.

GRACE

I was overcome last night.—How did it happen, C?

CECELIA

The new job didn't pan out. Tom ran into him somewhere and telephoned to ask if he could bring him out for a day or two, he'd been ill. There was nothing to do but say yes. Now, of course, he wants to keep him.

GRACE

Why not—you know—just give him something, and—?

CECELIA

He won't take anything without earning it. Tom swears he'll teach him manners—at least to the extent of calling us "Sir" and "Madam." He said it was the one birthday-present he really— (*She sees* REGAN *standing, beaming, in the doorway.*) Oh.

REGAN

Did someone *ring?*

CECELIA

Several times. Will you bring some hot coffee, please?

REGAN

Sure thing.

[*He takes the coffee-pot and goes out with it.*

[GRACE *laughs.*

GRACE

Manners!

CECELIA

I'm afraid he's hopeless.

GRACE

You know, I can't get over old Rufus K. actually sending checks. He can be nice, can't he?

CECELIA

Extremely. Did I tell you? He's invited us to spend the winter with him in town.

GRACE

Not in the big house?

CECELIA

Yes.

GRACE

But it's the most unheard-of thing I've ever heard of!

CECELIA

We may not go. Tom's not too keen for that, either.

GRACE

He's mad!—Of course you can persuade him. It will

be such— (TOM *comes down the stairs, a trifle white and wan.*) Ah! Good morning, host!

TOM

Is it?—How are you, Grace? Hello, Owen. (*He seats himself and eyes the food distrustfully.*) Did Franc get her train?

CECELIA

I imagine so.

TOM

I meant to get up. Where are Joe and Daisy?

CECELIA

They went walking.

[TOM *settles back painfully in his chair.*

GRACE

Oh come now! It's not as bad as that.

TOM

Lady, you don't know. (*To* CECELIA.) Was I dreadful?

CECELIA

You were delightful.

TOM

Oh, don't say that!—That means I put on an act.

GRACE

You were the life of the party.

[TOM *cringes.*

TOM

Good Grace.

[REGAN *comes in with the coffee-pot and a glass of what appears to be milk.*

REGAN (*heartily*)
How're'ye, Tom, my boy!

TOM

—'Morning, Red.
[REGAN *puts the coffee-pot upon the serving-table.* TOM *looks guiltily at* CECELIA, *who turns away.* REGAN *comes beaming from the serving-table, the glass in hand.*

REGAN
Look what Baby brought you—
[TOM *rises and goes to him.*

TOM

—Just a minute. (*He puts his arm through his, turns him away from the others and low enough to be heard by no one but him, murmurs:*) Look, Red—if you don't mind, I think you'd better be "Regan" from now on, and us "Sir" and "Madam."—You're a pretty good actor.
[REGAN *stiffens into the Perfect Butler.*

REGAN (*audibly*)
Right, Sir. H'I knows me place, Sir.
[TOM *laughs, and returns to the table.*

TOM
Don't lay it on.

REGAN

Oh no, Sir.

[*He offers the glass obsequiously.* TOM *takes it.*

GRACE

Milk?!

TOM

—Punch. (*He makes a face over it and returns it to* REGAN.) Could you possibly brush the nutmeg off?

REGAN

I think so, Sir.

TOM

Try. Move heaven and earth.

[REGAN *returns to the serving-table with the glass and removes the nutmeg.* DAISY *comes in from the hall.*

GRACE

Oh, hello!

DAISY

Good morning.

CECELIA

How was the walk?

DAISY

Very pleasant, thanks. We went miles. It's a lovely village.

CECELIA

It is nice.

DAISY

Whose house is the pretty white one on the Square?

CECELIA

Near the Post Office? (*To* GRACE.) Isn't that Judge Evans's?

GRACE

Yes.

DAISY (*to* TOM)

I hope you remembered to find the new magazine-proofs for me.

[TOM *takes some folded proof-sheets from his pocket.*

TOM

Right here.

[DAISY *extends her hand.*

DAISY

Please—

TOM

If you'd really like to—

DAISY

I should, very much.

[*She takes the proofs and goes to the stairs, where she seats herself upon the bottom step.* REGAN *returns the glass* of *punch to* TOM.

TOM

That's better.

[JOE *comes in from the hall.* REGAN *coughs discreetly behind his hand.*

REGAN (*not presuming to look directly at his master*)
Beg pardon, Sir—

TOM
Yes?

REGAN
—If I may say so, Sir—it has always seemed to me
that life is like a sailboat—

TOM (*smiling*)
Ah?

REGAN
In good weather, no better ridin' anywhere—but the
very deuce, Sir, in a storm, Sir.
[TOM *laughs and waves him away.*

TOM
Get out!
[REGAN *bows gravely.*

REGAN
Very good, Sir.
[*And goes out.* CECELIA's *fixed smile leaves her face.
She takes a deep breath.* DAISY *laughs softly,* JOE
loudly. GRACE *turns to* JOE.

GRACE
Oh hello!
[JOE *recovers himself and advances into the room.*

JOE
How are you?

GRACE

Pleasant walk?

JOE

If you like the country.

GRACE

I'll bet you made a good plot, too.

JOE

A good—?

GRACE

I know you writer-men!

DAISY (*from the stairs*)

—Remember your prescription for me, Tom?

TOM

Prescription?

DAISY

"The country's the place to work," you said.

JOE

Something did it for you, Daisy.

TOM

—Daisy herself.—You can spend the night, can't you, Joe?

JOE

It's up to Daisy.

DAISY

I'm not certain, yet. Must we say straight off?

CECELIA

Of course not.—Do, though. We'd so love having you.

TOM

I've got to run over to Greenwich to see one C. B. Williamson, but I'll be back this evening.

JOE

The publisher?

TOM

Yes. Why?

JOE

What have *you* got to do with that old pirate?

[TOM *smiles.*

TOM

Shh!—It's a secret.

[JOE *stares.*

JOE

My God!

GRACE

You're coming to my house for Sunday breakfast, you know.

JOE

Thanks, we've had it.

GRACE

Oh, but mine is a very special breakfast!—

JOE (*to* TOM)

—I liked the old Press building better.

TOM

We needed more room.

CECELIA (*to* TOM)

Don't you want some coffee or something?

TOM

This is fine. Will you join me in a milk-punch, Daisy?

DAISY

Would you mind awfully if I didn't?

TOM

I'm not sure.

GRACE

Not disapproving, is she?
[DAISY *laughs pleasantly.*

DAISY

Not in the least.

TOM (*to* JOE)

—You couldn't publish a magazine in that old shack.

JOE

Don't tell me it's that smart.

GRACE

I think it's going to be a sensation. I'm practically a collaborator, aren't I, Tom?
[TOM *laughs.*

TOM

Grace is my reaction-agent. She submits to tests.

[DAISY *stares at the proofs.*

DAISY

Is this all of it?

TOM

—The dummy for the first number.

DAISY

No name yet—

TOM

No.

JOE

—Any Sunday papers, by any *chance?*

TOM

—In the living-room. I'll send for them.

JOE

It's all right. I'll read them there.

[*He goes out.* TOM *looks after him.* GRACE *rises.*

TOM

Extraordinary fellow, Fisk.

GRACE

My people will be arriving. Who's going to run me home?

[*She holds out her hand to* TOM. *He takes it and rises.*

TOM

We'll go in Joe's Ford, and shock the village.

GRACE

Divine!

DAISY

Bring it back, Tom.

TOM

You bet.—How about your coming with us?

[DAISY *rises upon the stairs.*

DAISY

Thanks, but I want to finish this.

TOM

Be sure to like it.

DAISY

I'm afraid I'm no judge.

GRACE

Tom, I've got to tell you: *I* think the idea of a white roof in this country is idiotic.

[*She tucks his hand under her arm and they move toward the door.*

TOM (*as they go out*)

So do I. It's insane. Whatever made you think of it?

[DAISY *mounts the stairs and goes out,* CECELIA *watching her.* OWEN *moves toward the living-room.* CECELIA's *low voice stops him.*

CECELIA

Owen——

OWEN

What, C?

CECELIA

Why did she come?

OWEN

Daisy? I thought you wanted her, for all those highly special reasons.

CECELIA

—First she said she couldn't. Then she telephoned back she would.

OWEN

Well?

CECELIA

I believe she came for some special reason of her own.

OWEN

Quite possibly.

CECELIA

What, though?

OWEN

Search me.

CECELIA

Twice last night I caught her watching me in the most curious way. Once when I was with Fisk, once with you.—But you know, I'm not the least bit jealous any more. I'm even inclined to like her.

OWEN

That's big of you.

CECELIA

I suppose Fisk is one of hers, **too.**

OWEN (*frowning*)

How do you mean?

CECELIA

Sweet innocent!

OWEN

How's that?

CECELIA

I should think by this time you'd know a promiscuous little— (*She sees his frown deepen, and with a gesture, concludes:*)—Oh, well—

OWEN

You're a strange girl, C.—And a pretty cruel one.

CECELIA

—Not at all. I tell you I don't mind in the least. In fact I really don't see why Tom and she shouldn't be as good friends now as—well, as you and I are.

OWEN

Their history is a little different.

CECELIA

Why? Don't you like our history?

OWEN

What there is of it.—A trifle uneventful, don't you

think?—Or shall we simply call it lacking in excitement?

[*A moment. Then:*

CECELIA

—You've been so strange, lately. So remote, Owen.

OWEN

I wasn't aware of it.

CECELIA

—Refusing to help us one bit with Mr. Williamson.

OWEN

But Tom doesn't want to be helped!

CECELIA

I do.

OWEN

C, I've told you. I simply can't do it.

[CECELIA *turns from him coldly.*

CECELIA

Very well.

OWEN

Certainly, you must realize—

CECELIA

Of course. (*She moves toward the living-room*) Come on—shall we?

OWEN

I've told you a dozen times, I'm counsel for Williamson's, and—

[CECELIA *stops and turns to him.*

CECELIA

Exactly.—And so they do whatever you tell them to.

OWEN

Tom's price is out of all reason.

CECELIA

Not if they really want it.

OWEN

But hang it, he made it that to stand them off! He doesn't want them to have it.

CECELIA

Tom doesn't know what he wants. (*Coaxing.*)—Just one little word to them from you—on the telephone —before he goes over this afternoon—now—before he gets back from Grace's.

OWEN

There's something called legal ethics you seem not to understand, C.

CECELIA

And something called friendship? (*He turns away. A moment. Then she looks at him sideways.*) Owen— (*He gestures "What?"*) "Lacking in excitement," you said.—For you?

OWEN

For you, I meant.

CECELIA

I suppose you're the judge of that, too.

OWEN

I don't know who else.

CECELIA

Of course you couldn't possibly be wrong.

OWEN

Could I?

CECELIA (*softly*)

—And I'm not a human being at all, of course.
[*He advances toward her.*

OWEN

C—!

CECELIA (*quickly*)

Do one thing for me: just tell them it *might* be a
good thing for them.—It might, mightn't it?

OWEN

But even so, I—don't think I can.

CECELIA

—That it *is* high—admit that—but it might be a
good thing. (*He ponders it, frowning.*)—Owen—
telephone him—just one little word, Owen— (*He is
about to protest again, but is stopped by her even
gaze and her hand upon his arm. Finally he nods as-
sent. She breathes:*) You darling— (*He inclines
toward her, but she leans away from him. Suddenly
he glances up at the staircase. She senses that someone is coming, and begins to talk rapidly, in a different voice:*)—And of course it will be the most

marvellous thing for Tom if Williamson agrees. You can imagine what it will mean to him.

OWEN

Yes, of course.

[DAISY *comes down the stairs, the magazine-proofs still in hand.*

CECELIA

His father will be pleased as Punch, too, but the main thing is— (*She looks at* DAISY *in pretended surprise.*) Oh, hello! Owen and I were just talking about The Bantam Press combining with Williamson's. Owen engineered it.

OWEN

Oh no, C. If there's any credit due—

[CECELIA *laughs, and exclaims:*

CECELIA

Never mind! (*Then again, to* DAISY.)—I'm so excited about it, I can hardly speak. (*Then, to* OWEN.) —Why, Owen—do you realize?—But you wanted to telephone, didn't you?

OWEN

Why, er—why—yes, yes, I did.

[CECELIA *moves toward the living-room.*

CECELIA

It's in here, now. (*He follows. She speaks over her shoulder to* DAISY.) Coming along?

DAISY

In just a moment.

[OWEN *and* CECELIA *go out, encountering* JOE *coming in.* DAISY *gazes after them.*

JOE (*to* CECELIA)

I thought I'd get ready for breakfast—lunch—whatever it is.

CECELIA

But you look lovely!

[*She follows* OWEN *out, into the living-room.* DAISY *moves to the table, where she sits, staring in front of her, slowly comprehending.* JOE *approaches her, as* REGAN *comes in.*

JOE (*to* DAISY)

What do you say we— (REGAN *clears his throat portentously.*)—God, Red, get that fixed, will you?

[REGAN *lifts a lemon in two fingers.*

REGAN

Have you seen this one?

JOE

I had grapefruit.

REGAN

Give me a five-dollar bill. (JOE *finds one for him.* REGAN *folds it and closes his hand upon it.*) Which hand?

JOE

That one. (REGAN *opens both hands.* DAISY *is still staring, wrapt in thought.*) Good!—Only where does the lemon come in?

[REGAN *beckons him nearer, cuts the lemon with a*

fruit-knife, extracts a five-dollar bill from it, shows it to him, picks up a tray, and moves toward the door..

REGAN

Thank you, sir.

[*He goes out with the tray and* JOE'S *five dollars.* JOE *turns to* DAISY *about to speak, but she speaks first.*

DAISY

Are you packed, Joe?

JOE

Not yet. Why?

DAISY

I want to go.

JOE

What's the rush?

DAISY

I want to get out of this house.

JOE

But why all of a sudden?

DAISY

I want to get out, that's all.

JOE

Tom?

DAISY

Yes.

JOE

Poor devil—

DAISY

Yes.

JOE

Of course he's terribly on the defensive: you can see that.

DAISY (*dully*)

Can you?

JOE

Of course. He felt us disapproving, and simply gave us the works.

DAISY

Maybe.

JOE

He was awful last night, all right.

DAISY

Go and pack, Joe.

JOE

And what an outfit they were!—I give you Grace Macomber in your Christmas stocking.

DAISY

Thanks.

JOE

I'll even throw her husband in, for good measure.

DAISY

That would be too divine.

JOE

And all those pitiful second-hand opinions of Tom's! What's happened to him? What do you suppose has done it, for God's sake—

DAISY

That's what I came to find out.

JOE

Have you?

DAISY

Yes.

JOE

What?

DAISY

The most pitiful thing that can happen to any man.

JOE

But what?

DAISY

Go and pack, Joe.

JOE

It won't take a minute.—It certainly can't be C. *I* think she's a fine girl, don't you? I talked with her for quite awhile last night. She made great sense. I think she's a damned nice, attractive woman.

[DAISY *moves away from him.*

DAISY

So was Delilah.

JOE

Deli—? Oh come on, Daisy!

DAISY

—And bring my bag down with yours.

JOE

But I don't get you at all.

DAISY (*turning*)

Will you go and pack?

JOE

Honestly, Daisy, you're the damndest girl.

[TOM *comes in from the pantry, a whisky-and-soda in hand.*

TOM

A drink anyone?

JOE

At this hour? I should say not.

[TOM *seats himself at the end of the table, facing them.*

TOM

Too bad.

JOE

Besides, we've got to go.

TOM

So soon? Too bad. (*He takes a swallow of his drink, and smiles at them.*) Godspeed—

JOE (*After a moment*)

—There was a fellow once told me drink was in a way to becoming my own personal Hollywood—

TOM

Really? How amusing.

JOE

You, by a strange coincidence.

TOM

Oh not possibly!

JOE

—And it was you, incidentally, who taught me how to drink moderately.

TOM

No mean feat, I'm sure.

JOE (*With a gesture*)

Well, physician—

[TOM *raises his glass again, still smiling.*

TOM

Similia similibus curantur. Translated, the hair of the dog that—

DAISY

Go get ready, will you, Joe?

[JOE *stares at* TOM *a moment, then mounts the stairs and goes out.*

TOM

—So solemn—all so solemn. (*He puts down his glass, unfinished.*) I'm sorry you don't like my friends.

DAISY

Your—?

TOM

They are, however.—Did you read the magazine?

DAISY

Most of it.

TOM

Couldn't finish it, eh?

DAISY

No. I didn't care for it.

TOM

Why not?

DAISY

It seemed to me that one oh-so-bright weekly was enough, without more of the same.

TOM

—Not sufficiently solemn. I see.

DAISY

Not half!—And so. *cheap*, Tom! Oh, how can you? [*A moment. Then:*

TOM

You can't please everybody.

DAISY

Never mind. It doesn't matter.

[TOM *drops his cynical tone and speaks genuinely:*

TOM

Doesn't it, Daisy?

DAISY

Tom, ever since I got home I've heard from all sides how you've changed. I came here to find out if it was true, and if so why.

TOM

Well, is it?

DAISY

Tom—

TOM

And if so why? Why?

DAISY (*a sudden cry*)

Oh, Tom— I pity you with all my heart!
[*He is at her side in an instant, her wrists in his hands.*

TOM

Pity me! What are you talking about?

DAISY

I came to find out. I've found out. Now I'm going. (*She calls.*) Joe!

TOM

Found out what? Pity me why?
[DAISY *looks down at her wrists.*

DAISY

Would you mind? (*He releases her. A moment. They*

gaze at each other. Her eyes soften.)—And love you, Tom—love you with all my heart, as well. Remember that.

TOM (*brokenly*)

Daisy, I—(*He recovers himself, and with the recovery the cynical smile returns. He advances, one hand out, his voice coaxing.*) Give us a kiss, Daisy. [*She takes a step back from him, in horror. Her call is almost a scream:*

DAISY

Joe! Are you ready?

[JOE's *voice is heard from the stairs.*

JOE

Coming!

[JOE *comes down the stairs with the bags.* CECELIA *comes in from the living-room.*

CECELIA

Did someone call? (*She sees the bags.*) Why, what's all this?

DAISY

I'm sorry, but we've got to leave.

CECELIA

But what's happened?

DAISY

I suddenly remembered something. Please don't bother—

CECELIA

But I never heard of such a—

DAISY

I'm terribly sorry, but it can't be helped.

CECELIA

But can't you at least wait until after luncheon?

DAISY

I'm afraid not.

[*She turns to* JOE.

JOE (*to* CECELIA)

Good-bye. Thanks very much.

CECELIA

Good-bye. I must say it all seems very strange. (*Then to* DAISY.)—And when we've so loved having you.

DAISY

You were kind to ask us.

CECELIA

Well, if you insist, I suppose there's no help for it. Good-bye. Do come again when you can really stay. —Your coat's here, isn't it?

[*She goes out into the hall.*

JOE

Give me a ring sometime, Tom.

TOM

Right.

[JOE *looks at* DAISY. *She nods her head in the direction of the door. He goes out.*

DAISY

Good-bye, Tom.

TOM

—Once I wouldn't say it, would I?

DAISY

Once you wouldn't—

TOM

Well, good-bye.

DAISY

—This time you do.—

TOM

Good-bye.

[*She gestures helplessly, turns and goes out. For a moment he is alone. A door is heard to close, then* CECELIA *re-enters.*

CECELIA

Honestly! If that wasn't the rudest thing! (*He is silent.*)—I presume you agree, don't you?

TOM

I don't know what it was.

[*He stares in front of him, unseeing. She looks at him intently for a moment. Then:*

CECELIA

Well—if we're going to Grace's—

TOM

I'll get my hat.

[*He moves toward the hall. She follows.*

CURTAIN

ACT THREE

SCENE II

At TOM COLLIER'S. *Ten o'clock the same night.*

The dining-room is dimly lighted from the hall and living-room. There is a small fire burning in the fire place. Leaves have been removed from the table, which is now at its smallest. Two chairs are at the table, the others against the wall.

REGAN *comes in from the hall with an armful of wood, some of which he places upon the fire, making it burn brighter. This done, he lights a small candle-lamp upon the table. Two places have been set and a light supper prepared: a platter of cold meat, a bowl of salad, sandwiches, fruit. There is a champagne glass at each place. A moment, then* CECELIA *calls from up-stairs:*

CECELIA

Regan?

REGAN

—Right here, Ma'am.

CECELIA

I thought I heard a car.

REGAN

Yes, Madam.

CECELIA

Is Mr. Collier's supper ready?

REGAN

Yes, Madam.

[*He lights a small lamp on the serving-table, pokes the fire again, and goes out into the hall. A moment, then* CECELIA *comes down the stairs, in another charming negligee, this time more severe in cut and somber in color. She examines the table, rearranges a few things and puts out the lamp upon the serving-table. Now the room is lit only by the candle-lamp and the fire upon the hearth. A door closes in the hall. She turns toward it, calling:*

CECELIA

Tom?

[TOM *comes in.*

TOM

Hello. (*He looks at the table.*) What's all this?

CECELIA

I thought you might be hungry. I know what you think of Williamson's food. (*He looks at the fire, then around him, curiously.*) What's the matter?

TOM

—Lighted this way, it reminds me of some place.

CECELIA

Where?

TOM

I don't know.

[*His voice is strange, as if speaking from a distance.*

CECELIA

Do eat something, dear.

[*Again he looks about him, puzzled.*

TOM

—I came back the long way, over the Pound Ridge road, through Middle Patent.

CECELIA

What made you do that, Silly—

TOM

I don't know, I wanted to drive.

[*Now it is her he looks at curiously.*

CECELIA

Tom—what *is* the matter?

[*He shakes his head, as if to shake something out of it, and laughs shortly.*

TOM

Sorry!

CECELIA (*anxiously*)

Everything went all right, didn't it?

TOM

Oh yes, perfectly. (*A moment. Then:*) In fact, it's settled.

CECELIA

Not already!

TOM

Yes. They've signed. All I have to do is to dig up a

notary in the Village and write my name under theirs.

CECELIA

Oh, Tom!

TOM

Are you pleased?

CECELIA

Aren't you?

TOM

I think something's happened to my nervous system. I feel awfully light.

CECELIA

You're famished. Come and sit down and eat— (*She draws him to the table. He seats himself there, and for a moment drops his head in his hands.*)—And tired, too, poor darling.

TOM

No—just light. So awfully light.—Thinking too much.

[*She puts meat and salad upon a plate and sets it before him.*

CECELIA

Here.

TOM

C—

CECELIA

Yes, dear?

TOM

I think it's time we had a child or two, C.
[*A moment. Then:*

CECELIA

We'll talk about that.

TOM

Yes. We must. (*Another moment.*)—The trees along
the road stood out like—(*He rubs his eyes and looks
up again.*)—like whatever it is trees stand out like.

CECELIA

You've been going much too hard, you know.

TOM

It's good for me. I'm having visions. (*Again he looks
around him.*)—What *is* it it reminds me of?
[*She seats herself near him at the table.*

CECELIA

—Nothing. You're just tired and hungry.

TOM

Please let me have my visions. (REGAN comes in with
a pint of champagne.) Good evening, Mr. Regan.

REGAN

Good evening, Sir.

TOM

—Those buttons on your coat—you know, they're
terribly bright.

REGAN

I'll try to bring 'em down.

TOM

Do. It's essential.—Champagne, is it?

CECELIA

I thought you might feel like celebrating.

TOM

Well—

CECELIA

A little wine won't hurt you, Tom.

TOM (*to himself*)

—The little more, and how much it is— (*Rousing himself.*)—Fill them, Mr. Regan. (REGAN *looks at him oddly, then fills the glasses.* TOM *raises his and squints at it.*)—Infinite riches, in a little room.

[CECELIA *laughs.*

CECELIA

You've got the quotes badly.

TOM

Little lamb, who made thee?—Regan—dost thou know who made thee? (*He holds out the glass to him.*)—And a little more, old son. (REGAN *refills the glass and goes out.* TOM *watches him, curiously.*)— The discreet withdrawal—I've seen that before, too. (*Looks around him again, then cries, suddenly:*) I know! The Florentine!—A private room at the Florentine.

CECELIA

What's that?

TOM

A kind of a hotel. Flora Conover's place.

CECELIA

It sounds wicked.

TOM

It used to be the best twenty-guinea house in London.

CECELIA

Twenty-guinea? What are you talking about?

TOM

In advance, at that.

[CECELIA *glances at him.*

CECELIA

Rather expensive, wasn't it?

TOM

But one went to Flora's to celebrate.—And the food was good, the waiter discreet, the wines excellent, the lady most artful.

CECELIA

Tom! How revolting—

TOM

But we must send the boys back happy, you know.

CECELIA

I don't care to hear about it, thank you.

TOM

Very well, my dear.

[*A moment. He stares at his glass. Then:*

CECELIA

Weren't they difficult at all, Tom?

TOM

Who? Williamson's?—Easy.

CECELIA

And you actually got your own terms?

TOM

Except for their *r*ight to pass on my selections.

CECELIA

That's probably just a form.

TOM

Probably.

CECELIA

They want to feel they have *some* say.

TOM

That's all.—C, what have you done to your hair?

CECELIA

Why, nothing, why?

TOM

It looks lighter.

CECELIA

It isn't.

[*He gazes at it for a moment longer, then eats a little, disinterestedly.*

TOM

I quashed the announcement they'd prepared for the papers.

CECELIA

Why? What was it?

TOM

"Williamson, Warren and Company have absorbed The Bantam Press, formerly owned by——"

CECELIA

"Absorbed"!

TOM

Yes. Like a sponge. I quashed it. For "absorbed" read "bought a controlling interest in."

CECELIA

Well—that's more like it.

TOM

—Poor little Bantam.—For "Bantam" read small little, plucked little capon.

CECELIA

Oh, don't, Tom! You know it's a good thing for you —it's a grand thing for you.

TOM

—Increased scope.

CECELIA

Of course.

TOM

—Perfect distribution facilities.

CECELIA

But aren't they?

TOM

Williamson, Warren Books Girdle the Globe. Hear
the eagle scream.—Poor little Bantam—peep,
peep—

CECELIA

—And I thought you'd be beside yourself for joy.
[*He gazes at her. She is.*

TOM

C, your eyes are so bright.
[*She laughs shortly.*

CECELIA

Eat, you. You're seeing things.
[*He looks at his plate.*

TOM

C—

CECELIA

Yes, dear?

TOM

—Little love is no love.

CECELIA

—Meaning what, precisely?

'OM

It wasn't necessary to lock your door against me last
night.

[*A moment. Then:*

ECELIA

But I didn't.—I mean—not against—

'OM

Then why?

ECELIA

I'm—it's just that sometimes I'm afraid, alone at
night.

[*He is watching her.*

'OM

I don't believe you.

[*She laughs nervously.*

ECELIA

Well, really!

OM

I don't believe you, C. (*She averts her head.*)—Only
I'd like you to know that that isn't necessary, ever.

ECELIA

Very well.

[*Suddenly he reaches for her hand and takes it.*

OM

Why was it? Tell me instantly why it was.

ECELIA

Is that an order?

TOM

Tell me.

[*She tries to meet his gaze, but cannot.*

CECELIA (*with difficulty*)

You mean—why I—why I didn't want you near me—

TOM

Yes.

CECELIA

—And you don't know—

TOM

No.

CECELIA

Well, if you don't, you ought to.

TOM

Tell me, I say.

CECELIA

You'd been so—consistently disagreeable, that's all.

TOM

About what?—Wanting Regan back?

CECELIA

No.

TOM

What, then?

CECELIA

Your father, chiefly. (*She rises and goes to the serving-table.*) He telephoned this afternoon. (*A moment.*) He wanted to know if you'd got the birthday-check. (*Another moment.*) I told him that you had, and had tried to call him. (*He turns away.*) Well, I had to say something!

[*She reseats herself at the table with a plate for herself.*

TOM

I don't know whether to send it back, or just not to cash it.

[*He finds a check among the letters in his pocket, and looks at it, frowning.*

CECELIA

—Of course, you simply can't allow yourself to show any kind of graciousness toward him.

TOM

No.

CECELIA

—As a way of telling you how pleased with you he is, he sends you a small check,—and you have the extraordinary bad taste to—(*He holds the check out for her to see. Her eyes widen.*) What!—Good heavens— I don't believe it!

TOM

There it is.

CECELIA

But there isn't that much money in the world!

TOM

In Father's world there is. He feels he can afford it, to get us to come and live with him.

CECELIA

Of course, I don't understand your attitude about that, either.

TOM

Don't you, C?

CECELIA

He knows how inconvenient it is here in winter,—and having that great, huge, lovely house in town, it's perfectly sweet and natural of him to—to, well to ask—

TOM

Yes—you, to preside night after night at his deadly dinners, me to listen eternally to his delphic advice on what to do and how to live—in short, to allow him to own us. Of course, he's willing to pay. He always is.

CECELIA

Oh, how ridiculous you are, really!—His whole life long he's tried to help you, to do things for you—

TOM

—In order to own me. I tell you I know him.

CECELIA

You're the only child he's got, and he's an old man and a very lonely man. I think it's horrible beyond belief, the way you treat him. How you can be so hard, I don't know.

TOM

Hard!—I'm not hard enough. All my life I've been

trying to harden. I was born soft, that's the trouble with me.

CECELIA

You soft!

TOM

Yes. Born it.—And then brought up to refuse to face any truth that was an unpleasant truth, in myself or anyone else—always be the little gentleman, Tommy —charming and agreeable at all costs—give no pain, Tommy.

CECELIA

You seem to have outgrown it nicely.

TOM

Not yet, I haven't. No, not by a long shot. The inclination's still there, all right. Still going strong.

CECELIA

But don't be discouraged.

TOM (*wearily*)

All right, C.

CECELIA

—It's nothing but your old self-consciousness about money, again. It simply defeats me.—Honestly, has everyone who lives well sold his soul to the devil?

TOM (*rising*)

"Lives well"!—I'd give my eyes to live well. That's all I want for us.

[*He goes to a chair at the window.*

CECELIA

Oh—definitions again.—We being so weak, of course, that a little luxury would completely ruin us.

TOM

—Little—little—everything's so little. Add it up, though. (*His head sinks upon his breast.*)—Add it up.

CECELIA

To my way of thinking, if a person can't stand—

TOM

Let's drop it.

CECELIA (*coldly*)

Very well. We shall.

[*He looks up again.*

TOM

—Now you've gone from me again—

CECELIA

A lot you care.

TOM

Oh C—my lovely C— Where are you? What's become of you?

CECELIA

There's something you call your damned integrity—

[TOM *rises from his chair.*

TOM (*suddenly, sharply*)

That's the word!

[CECELIA *rises also.*

CECELIA

I see it's no use talking.

[*A silence. He looks at her intently.*

TOM

—This is what you call "being disagreeable."

CECELIA

Yes. Very.

[*He returns to her.*

TOM

—But how to be otherwise, when—

CECELIA (*in a burst*)

Possibly by being the fine, kind, generous man you ought to be!

TOM

To Father?

CECELIA

You might begin there.

TOM

—Accept the check with thanks—and go to live with him—

CECELIA

It's only for a few months—and I think to refuse his present would be extremely bad manners—just about in a class with those of your little lady of easy virtue, this morning. If— (*She sees she has gone too far.*) I'm sorry to have said that about her. I didn't mean—

TOM

Never mind. (*A long moment. Then:*)— Suppose I should do as you say about Father—

CECELIA

Oh, Tom—do be the darling I know you are!

TOM

Would you like me better?

CECELIA

Much.

TOM

How much?

CECELIA

Oh—very much.

[*He leans forward, watching her, hardly believing it possible.*

TOM

No locked doors, anymore?

CECELIA (*lowly*)

Not one—ever—

TOM

That sounds—most inviting.

[*She smiles.*

CECELIA

Does it?

[*Again he seats himself at the table.*

TOM

—And suddenly I'm beginning to see with an awful clearness—

[*He stops.*

CECELIA (*smiling*)

What? How stupid you've been?—And what I am to you?

TOM (*after a moment*)

Yes.

CECELIA

—And so you *are* going to be nice again?

TOM

You'll see.

(*Again* CECELIA's *smile.*

CECELIA

—But how am I to be sure?

TOM

You've told me ways to convince you.

CECELIA

I do so hate us not to agree, Tom.

TOM

I know.

[*She brings her chair closer and sits at his side.*

CECELIA

I want so to feel—I don't know—together again, as we used to be.

[*Once more,* TOM *looks incredulously around him, at the room. Then:*

TOM

You're very pretty, you know—

CECELIA

Why, thank you, Sir.

TOM

—Very exciting, too.

[*His manner has changed. From now on, he is no longer the husband sitting before the fire with his wife, but a host at supper with a pretty girl, whom later he will know better.*

CECELIA

I don't know whether it's you or the wine speaking.

TOM

—Me.

CECELIA

Shall we have a little more?

TOM

Why not?

[*She presses the button.*

CECELIA

It's a party, then.

TOM

It's a party.

CECELIA

Sometimes you're so thrilling, Tom.

TOM

You think?

[*A moment. Then:*

CECELIA

Put your arms around me, Tom—

[*He inclines toward her, does not touch her, b
looks full into her eyes, searching for something
still cannot believe he will find.*

TOM

Are they around?

CECELIA (*in a breath*)
Oh—yes—yes—

[REGAN *comes in.*

TOM

Another small bottle.

[REGAN *goes out.* CECELIA *laughs a little throaty, e
cited laugh.*

CECELIA

We shouldn't. You know we shouldn't.

TOM

But we seem to be—

CECELIA

I feel—all at once I feel terribly naughty, somehow-

TOM

I suppose you're the prettiest girl I've ever seen-

CECELIA (*archly*)

So nice of you to think so, Sir.

TOM

—So very attractive—

CECELIA

I like to be attractive.

TOM

So very seductive—

CECELIA

There, there! That's enough!

[*He has found it. Coldly he salutes it:*

TOM

You're a strange woman. Your lips drop honeycomb, your mouth is smoother than oil.

CECELIA

Now what are you quoting?

[REGAN *comes in with the wine.*

TOM

—Give the lady some, waiter. (REGAN *fills* CECELIA's *glass, then* TOM's, *without a word.*) You can leave the bottle. (REGAN *places it upon the table, near him.*) —And that will be all. (REGAN *bows and goes out.* CE-CELIA *raises her glass and smiles invitingly. He raises his, murmuring:*)—To the pleasant ways of life.

[*She drinks. He does not.*

CECELIA

—Such pleasant ways.

[*She smiles at her glass.*

TOM

Is it good?

CECELIA

So good.—I'm feeling it a little.

TOM

That's what it's for, eh?

CECELIA

It must be.

TOM

"Champagne, the friend of lovers"—

[*Her face inclines to him, then she averts her head.*

CECELIA (*softly*)

No—not yet—

TOM

Artful child.

CECELIA

You think?

TOM

—Lovely, alluring thing—

CECELIA

I like you too, now.

TOM

Pleasant here, isn't it?

CECELIA

So pleasant. (*She refills her glass and finds that his is still full.*)—But you aren't taking any—

TOM

It makes me see almost too clearly.

CECELIA

Take a little more, and everything will get so—lovely and vague and—the way I feel now.

TOM

—A good feeling, is it?

CECELIA (*a whisper*)

Delicious— (*She gropes for his hand, holds it against her breast.*) Oh—Tom— (*He looks at her. She smiles again.*)—One last toast? (*He draws her to her feet, glass in hand.*) But to what—what to?

TOM

You name it.

[*A moment. Then:*

CECELIA

To love— (*She comes against him, steadies her glass in both hands against his breast, bends her head and takes it. He raises his glass, holds it for a moment near his lips, then sets it down, untouched, upon the table. She replaces hers beside it, and murmurs:*) And darling—

TOM

Yes?

CECELIA

You—you *are* going to be an angel about—about things, aren't you?

TOM

You'll see.

CECELIA

Oh, I knew you would!—I'm so happy— (*She smiles,
moves slowly toward the stairs, and mounts them,
opening the door at the top. There she turns and
whispers.*) Don't be long—

[*And goes out.* TOM'*s eyes following her. Then he
turns and stares down at the table. Finally his hand
finds the bell and presses it. A moment, then* REGAN
enters, in a business suit.

TOM

See here, Red, I—

REGAN (*sharply*)

Never mind! (TOM *looks up.* REGAN *gestures.*) All I
mean is—well, I'm out for good, this time.

TOM

Why?

REGAN

I just don't like it here, that's all.

TOM

When do you want to go?

REGAN

As soon as I can.

TOM

To-night, then.

REGAN

That's all right with me. I'm packed.

TOM

Look in and say good-bye as you're leaving.

REGAN

I'm leaving now.

TOM

Look in, anyhow. (REGAN *turns to go.*)—Have you got a fountain-pen? (REGAN *finds a pen and gives it to him.*)—Don't let me forget to return it. (REGAN *goes out. Slowly, methodically,* TOM *opens the pen, shakes it, spreads the check upon the table and writes upon its back. Then, as carefully, he replaces the top of the pen, picks up the check and waves it back and forth, to dry it.* REGAN *re-enters with a traveling-bag.* TOM *returns the pen to him.*)—Here you are. Thanks.

REGAN

Well—good-bye—

TOM

Get into the car.

REGAN

I can walk to the train all right.

TOM

Bring my coat and hat, will you? (REGAN *does not stir.*)—Will you bring my coat and hat, please? (REGAN *puts down his bag and goes into the hall for them.* TOM *folds the check carefully, goes to the fire*

*place and places it upon the mantelpiece, one corner
under a vase.* REGAN *re-enters with his overcoat and
hat.* TOM *puts on the hat.* REGAN *holds the coat for
him.* TOM *gets into it. He takes a cigarette from the
pocket and puts it in his mouth.*)

REGAN

What's the idea?

TOM

—Light, please— (REGAN *holds a match for him.*
TOM *pulls on his gloves.*) Now, then—

REGAN

I can walk, I tell you.

TOM

Not at all. We'll drive in.

REGAN

We will—?

TOM (*very gently*)

I'm going back to my wife, Red.

REGAN

To your—?

[*Puzzled,* REGAN *looks toward the lighted doorway
at the top of the stairs.*

TOM

—To my wife, I said.

[REGAN *picks up his bag, and goes out, into the hall.*
TOM *looks once around him, draws a deep breath of
smoke, exhales it slowly, then turns and follows him.*

CURTAIN

WS - #0082 - 081121 - C0 - 229/152/11 - PB - 9780243475308 - Gloss Lamination